JOHN McGRATH
RESPONSE DOG

© John McGrath 2015
Steve Stone has asserted his rights under the Copyright, Design and Patents Act, 1988, to be identified as the author of this work.
Published by Digital Dreams Publishing 2015

FOREWORD

When they say, "a dog is man's best friend," it is so true, especially when you work with a dog and rely on them to help keep you safe. They really are a hundred percent loyal and trustworthy. The bond you develop between yourself and a dog is a strong one, one that lasts for years. Even though sadly, we outlive our dogs several times over. A dog brings so much pleasure and joy into your life, offering unconditional love and affection. They do require a lot of love and attention back - most dogs never like to be far from your side. But, you will have a friend for life, one of the most loyal friends you will ever have. Having a dog will reduce your stress levels and help you keep fit - by virtue of a dog needing to be taken for a walk. They are not for everyone though, and your lifestyle may preclude having a dog. Like any pet, having a dog is a responsibility and they do require looking after and plenty of attention. It is a sad fact that far too many dogs end up in rescue centres; discarded by owners who can no longer care or cope with their dog.

The UK, is a nation of dog and animal lovers, one that has never ceased to make me feel proud as a fellow dog owner and animal lover. There are so many concerned and thoughtful members of the public who will phone in to report a suffering animal. Be it a pet or a wild animal such as a fox, swan or badger. I have chased swans up and down a main road, tended an injured fox and sadly removed a dead badger from a road. I have to applaud the RSPCA, who have on many an occasion come to the rescue of an injured animal, no matter what day or time it is. I do hope this book will give you a greater insight into the work of police dogs as well as being entertaining, educational and insightful. Without police dogs, more criminals would get away, more police officers would be injured. Police dogs are every bit as important as a police car or a police helicopter. They may be classed as a resource, but they are so much more than that, they are fellow police officers, fellow crime fighters that never fail to execute their duties and step forward in a time of crisis, as this story will tell.

After all, who can resist a puppy with its puppy dog's eyes looking up at you, wanting to be cuddled and given some fuss, then watching that puppy grow. Training a puppy to become your best friend and partner in fighting crime on the thin blue line. This pretty much sums up being a police dog handler. The job has gotten harder as more and more a consideration about the use of force on a suspect. For each and every dog bite there is usually a payout, as it is cheaper to pay out compensation to a burglar than the costs of it going to court and the justification for the dog biting someone defended. This may seem bizarre to the public, but that is the way it is at this point in time. To the point that dogs are taught to bite once and hold on rather than multiple bites. Modern day policing has changed radically over the last few years, and who knows what the long term future of costly police dogs is? The police are changing not just due to austerity measures, but changes to the crimes themselves, with cybercrime being on an exponential rise. After all it is easier to rob a bank from behind a computer than to rush in armed with a shotgun. Better still, hold hundreds of thousands of people to ransom by locking their computer, mobile phone or tablet with spoof spyware or a virus hidden in a file or some free downloadable software. However, nothing can beat the ability of a dog's nose to track criminals, find drugs, guns and explosives, even with some of the latest high tech detection kit.

John McGrath January 2015

Back to School

I could hear Jet, my four year old German Shepherd police dog in the boot tapping his rather large paws, along with a slight growl and the odd snort as we made our way to our next job. Job is police speak for an incident. Jet always got excited as we travelled to a job - like a teenager on a first date. As we raced along with blue lights flashing and sirens wailing. He knew this meant we had got given something to do - Jet always hoped it involved him. At four years old, Jet had become not only my partner but my best friend as well. He was about average size for a German Shepherd, but had a ferocious bite and bark. Which had sent other police dogs on a few occasions cowering behind their handler.

Jet was half way through his working life of 7½ to 8 years. We knew what each other was thinking, Jet's very expressive face and eyes always gave away what jet was feeling too, excited, afraid, angry, in need of attention. Anyone who has a dog will know how you learn to read your dog and know exactly what they are thinking. As they say "your eyes are the window to your soul" the same is true of dogs. Look into a dog's eyes and they will tell you an awful lot about their personality and what they are thinking.

My wife on many occasions has complained that I give Jet more attention than her. Maybe I do, but we are together virtually 24 hours a day, seven days a week. With that becomes strong bond – I depend on Jet just as much as he depends on me.

The dog section I work in has 20 handlers, the mainstay of our dogs being German Shepherd. We have a small number of Cocker Spaniels, for drugs, money, weapon and cadaver searches. The handler's I work with most are Chris "Crane" due to his tall, thin physic, which one offender thought he looked like a tower crane and the name stuck. He is a giant beanpole who seems to always wind me up, Mark "Frenchy" due to hating the French and the section had to give him a nickname that would wind him up. Is a quiet and reflective man, but get him angry and then it's a different manner, his soft Scottish accent turns into a roar. Finally, there is Jane or 'Dotty' as she is affectionately called. Not because she is dotty far from it - she is one of the best handlers on the team. But due to the fact that on every social we have been on she always wears something with dots on it. As for the dogs, there is Dano after Dano from Hawaii Five O, and the fact we get called Five O on many occasions. Dano is a two year old Cocker Spaniel trained to search for drugs and he is pretty much the best sniffer dog on the section. Next we have Bono, I let you guess which famous rock band that name is linked to. Bono is a six year old German Shepherd known for his ability to bite people. Especially other police officers when he is grumpy, which seems to be most of the time these days. He is an excellent working dog and a great 'thief taker.' Finally, there is Moti another German Shepherd named after the German Shepherd Moti, who took a bullet in 2007 for his family after trying to stop a masked intruder enter the house. After shooting Moti, the intruder ran off and Moti made a full recovery.

Our section offers 24 hour cover 7 days a week, although sometimes there may be just one dog and handler on duty for calls force wide. With other handlers abstracted to take part in scheduled raids or searches. Police dogs are a real important part of police work and have helped to track down and capture many offenders over the years, along with the seizure of millions of pounds worth of drugs. The dogs can track on what we call a hard or soft surface. In dry conditions a soft surface can retain a smell, detectable by a dog for around two hours compared to just 45 minutes on a hard surface. A dog's sense of smell is around a thousand times better than our sense of smell. To a dog each of us has a unique smell detectable by a dog. They can even detect fear, anxiety and sadness. We shed 50 million skin cells, each minute, these cells can be detected by a dog's nose. That is why we try to ensure as few officers as possible have contaminated an area. Which will confuse the dog and make it much harder to track. Even once trained, a dog like Jet continues to refine their ability to track.

The job we had been sent to was quite some distance from where the dog section was based at police headquarters. The police headquarters is situated at one end of the county, so it could be a long blue light run, if you were sent straight out to a 'job' the moment you booked on duty. Which was located at the other side of the county. The job we were being sent to, was for two potential burglars who had just broken into a village school and had made off. It was 4pm on a chilly but bright December day, the police helicopter had also been requested and was making its way to the scene. Local bobbies had already flooded the area around the school and tried to put a perimeter on to stop the offenders escaping.

I pressed down the accelerator of my Skoda Octavia VRS estate, with a woosh from the turbo, the car quickly built up speed, and then a slight jolt from the front wheel as it scrabbled out of a pot hole. These cars are perfect for fast and dog friendly transport – reliable and take the daily grind of being a fast response car. Although, you could use a tank of fuel in a nine or ten hour shift. The VRSs powerful turbo petrol engine being quite thirsty, when driven in a more spirited fashion. The VRS I drive is just the same as the one you could buy at a main dealer less the blue lights, Airwave radio and boot fitted out to safely carry two dogs in cages. A misconception or urban myth, is that the police are given tweaked or modified cars. In fact, nearly all police cars are standard ones straight off the production line. I remember Volvo offering a power upgrade on their D5 V70 for the police a few years back though.

It would take us about 20 minutes to get there from HQ - as long as we got through before the rush hour traffic started to build up. Other than the usual drivers not seeing us - the reason it is so important to never go through a red light above 5mph, the drive was uneventful. Talking of red traffic lights, a cop off of my old shift only last year went a bit quick through a set of traffic lights and hit a van, punting it into a lamppost causing the driver serious injury. The cop was prosecuted for dangerous driving, but managed to keep their job. They now will not drive with blue lights, even though their driving ban has passed.

We nosed our way through the late afternoon traffic before arriving at the scene. Jet must have known we had arrived as he started barking in an excited manner, police dogs just love to work and are never happier than being let out to track an offender. The thrill of the chase is just as exciting to them as it is to the cops themselves, myself included. The minute I lifted the tailgate to the VRS - Jet's eyes opened up wide with his usual excited look, as he looked up at me, which was followed with a whine and growl as he waited impatiently to be let out.

The German Shepherd, also known as a Rielle Alsatian, is a breed of dog that originated in Germany. The German Shepherd is a relatively new breed of dog, with its origin dating to 1899. As part of the Herding Group, the German Shepherd is a working dog developed originally for herding and guarding sheep. Because of its strength, intelligence and abilities in obedience training, it is often employed in police and military roles around the world.

German Shepherds are highly active dogs and described in breed standards as self-assured. The breed is marked by a willingness to learn and an eagerness to have a purpose. They are curious, which makes them excellent guard dogs and suitable for search missions. German Shepherds have a loyal nature and bond well with people they know, most markedly with the one person to whom they consider the alpha of the household. This is very important as they are bred to protect those in their pack and feel stressed if they do not have a 'master'. However, they can become over-protective of their family and territory, especially if not socialised correctly.

They are not inclined to become immediate friends with strangers. German Shepherds are highly intelligent and obedient. Jet had all these characteristics; he was very protective of me both on and off duty. He had another four years of working life left before he would be retired and a new dog trained to fill Jet's paws on the section. The majority of police dogs in the world are German shepherds, although Labrador retrievers and several other breeds (like Breston, a Belgian Malinois is sometimes used, depending on what duties they will undertake.

With Jet out the back of the car and his longer tracking lead on, I led Jet to the area that the offenders were believed to be hiding. The police helicopter circling at 500 feet above had not been able to find them, even using its infrared camera, they had not been detected yet. As I got close, Jet began to get more excited and had picked up a track, his glossy black coat shimmering in the last rays of autumn sunshine as dusk fell. The name Jet had come from his larger than average swath of glossy black fur on his back.

  Jet picked up the pace as the scent got stronger and he headed up to a wall, a cop had just jumped over, when I shouted for them to get back over as the dog was going in. They scrambled back over the wall as if their life depended on it! The police helicopter was buzzing overhead like an annoying wasp unable to find anyone suspicious trying to lie low. I helped Jet over the wall and he leapt down whilst I quickly scrambled over the 5 foot tall, brick wall. Jet turned left and headed towards some large bushes, before he began barking wildly. I moved towards where Jet was barking and could make out the shape of a person hiding in the bushes. I ordered them out, saying "Come on out, or I will send the dog in." With a rustle from the bushes a black male appeared, looking quite dishevelled, saying "don't set the dog on me, don't set the dog on me, I will come quietly." Sure enough he did come quietly looking quite fearful of Jet, as I lead him to another officer to be handcuffed. I then gave Jet his reward, in the form of a bog standard green tennis ball, which Jet has to run and fetch, followed by plenty of praise.

  The intimidating growl of a well-trained German shepherd can cause many criminals to surrender instead of running or fighting. Which is much safer for all of those involved be it the criminal, a police officer or general public. The very presence of a police dog can prevent physical altercations. When a conflict does arise, dogs like Jet are faster and stronger than a police officer. Jet can catch a fleeing criminal and clamp down with his powerful jaws to apprehend the suspect until I manage to catch up. More often than not the offender is screaming for me to get the dog off. Sadly, a few do lash out and try to punch, kick or even worse stab the dog holding onto their leg or arm. Over the years police dogs have been injured in the line of duty.

Jet then continued to look for the other male, who had been described as a white male in his late teens in a dark coloured jacket and tracksuit bottoms. Jet seemed to pick up another track and was off this time over another wall and into a field. The field was quite soggy underfoot and my clean black boots, were soon covered in mud, as was Jet, who was now going to require a bath. Jet is not a dog who particularly likes being bathed, more often than not - I end up getting wetter than Jet does! He tends to leap out of the bath or shower, before I have time to stop him, then shake off all the water, with water flying off in all directions. Leaving me and the rest of the bathroom soaking. I have tried to wash him outside and hose him down, Jet just chewed though the hose pipe sending water flying in all directions and soaking me. My punishment for trying to wash him off with cold water...

The Police helicopter was still buzzing just above, seeing if it could follow ahead the direction of travel Jet was taking. As Jet came to a fence, he stopped and started sniffing around. This was usually an indication that Jet had lost the track and we went back slightly to see if we could pick the trail back up, but to no avail. I was disappointed only to have only found one of the offenders, but the one we had caught my 'cough' at interview and reveal who his partner in crime was.

This is the frustration of police work, sometimes you get your 'man' and sometimes you do not. Usually, if you have not caught them on one occasion you more than likely will on another. Many criminals are career criminals, trying to earn a living or feeding a drug habit. Some, like one burglar, who removed tiles from roofs and smashed his way through the loft ceiling. Burgled for the buzz and never actually stole anything. The damage he did to over thirty houses and the suffering and misery he brought to victims all for a buzz, I suppose makes it even worse. Not that anyone who has been burgled has not suffered. This is the part that criminals don't ever really consider. The impact of their crimes on the victim, be it a burglary, assault, or theft. Many, sadly, don't care and won't ever care. You have to remind yourself sometimes as a police officer that the decent law abiding people outweigh the criminals, some of whom are very nasty pieces of work. You spend most of your career as a police officer dealing with the worst 10% of society.

Billy Burglar

I have been in the police service for fourteen years now. I had joined, with the one intention of becoming a dog handler. It has taken me three attempts to get in as a PC, and then a further two attempts, just to become a dog handler. Once I had joined up, I have loved every minute both as a response officer and now as a dog handler. My love of dogs has come from having grown up with dogs; I had a Bearded Collie called Amber as a child, and after she died my mum and dad had got a second one called Isla. Isla was not such a lady - she loved to get dirty and roll around in the mud the moment she got a chance. Everyone thought she was the Dulex dog, but the Dulex dog is an Old English Shepherd.

That love of dogs has stayed with me and I had initially wanted to become a vet, but had not managed to get the grades required for veterinary school, nor to be honest, was I ever going to achieve the grades required. So my choice was to become a dog handler in the armed forces or join the police. I decided to join the police, although was part way through the Army selection process, when I got the letter to say I had been accepted into the police and given a date to start my training to become a police officer. The training was mentally tough, with frequent knowledge checks throughout my initial 20 weeks at Ryton, near Coventry. It was a residential course that I think works much better than the current 18 weeks non-residential at the force HQ.

I have loved virtually every minute of being a cop, there really is no other job like it. You have your good and bad days, sometimes going home with a real buzz. You meet some amazing people, both good and bad, whilst serving the public. The biggest issue I had with response and one of the other reasons I wanted to get into the dog section, was the never ending tide of paperwork. In the dog section we still have our fair share, but nothing like the amount, often in triplicate that I had, when I worked on response. Response are the police officers who respond to 999 calls and other non-emergency calls, ranging from antisocial behaviour to criminal damage and theft. The bit I miss though is being part of a rota and the camaraderie it brings, working with a Sgt and maybe three or four other cops. I haven't investigated in quite the same manner or depth either. Passing on that side to response cops or CID most of the time. If I had not become a dog handler I think I would have joined CID and become a detective.

About an hour into our shift, we got our first job of the night. A burglar had been reported as being seen entering a house and was believed to be still in the house. Police officers were already making their way into the area to put a cordon in place around the property. Jet and I would have the task of entering the house. Jet first, with myself following close behind. I could feel my own adrenaline starting to course through my veins. This was the type of job police officers live for. Where you catch someone in the process of committing a crime. In many ways this is why I joined up, to be a 'thief taker'. Jet could sense my excitement and in turn he got more excited than usual. Dogs do sense your mood and it can have an impact on their mood. If I am feeling down so is Jet, although he tries his best to cheer me up with a few licks and lying down at my feet. In some ways, having Jet, is like having a toddler that never grows up. This strapping German Shepard needs as much from me as I need from him.

With blue lights flashing away and the lights reflecting off shop windows giving the street a blue rinse effect I pressed on. The traffic was only light and we made good progress, making it to the scene in just over 10 minutes. I killed the blue lights and siren as I got close for a silent approach. Four other police cars were already in attendance. With cops standing round the perimeter of the house awaiting our arrival. Jet was anxious to get out and get stuck in, nearly pulling my arm off as he jumped out of the boot of the car and I grabbed his collar.

The local Sgt briefed me and showed me where the burglar had got in via the back kitchen window. He had forced the rear UPVC window open by removing the outside beading and taking the double glazed window pane out. It was perfect for me to lift Jet up and put him through before climbing through myself. The burglar could be clearly seen by police officers hiding at the front of the house. He was in what looked like the front bedroom wearing dark clothing. He had failed to notice that the police had surrounded the property.

I lifted Jet up and he scrabbled through the window before landing just to the left of the wooden kitchen table. He instantly picked up a scent and was off before I was fully through the window. He bolted upstairs with me in hot pursuit. As he entered the bedroom with the burglar in, the burglar tried to kick Jet and get away. Jets training kicked in and he bit the burglars arm hard. The burglar yelped, before shouting "get that fucking dog off, before I fucking kill it." I knew by his demeanour this burglar was not going to come quietly.

I pulled Jet off and shouted for assistance as Jet barked aggressively at the burglar. Two local bobbies rushed in and quickly cuffed the male to the rear before taking control of him. As he was taken downstairs, the burglar protested his innocence and said he had done nothing wrong. As we got close to the police van he started to kick off. Initially, just hurling abuse before he started to lash out and kick the two cops escorting him. Jet started to bark even louder and I warned the male I would set the dog on him if he did not calm down. This worked for a short period of time before he became more aggressive again. Four cops pushed him to the floor as gently as possible, before applying leg restraints, which are two Velcro straps that go round the ankle and just below the knee. In order to prevent the violent suspect kicking their legs out and injuring both himself and the cops escorting him.

Once in the van the burglar continued to shout and swear calling us all every name under the sun. I agreed to follow the van into custody just in case the burglar started to kick off again. With the recent closure of the nearest custody suite, we had to drive to the custody suite just outside the city centre. On arrival at the custody suite the male was still shouting and being aggressive. I got called a "bold fat fucker" due to the lack of hair on my head. Other cops trying to get him inside got similar names along with more protests of his innocence. Jet was in the car barking as he could hear the scuffle. We finally made it through the two custody doors and to the Custody Sgt's desk. The burglar now started making demands about phone calls and a drink before he would give any details. The custody Sgt was having none of this and the burglar became aggressive again. Custody Sgt told us to take him to a cell where he would have to have his clothes forcibly removed. The clothes would be needed for forensic examination. We had no choice but to cut his designer jeans off, along with his jacket and T-shirt. Leaving him to parade angrily around his cell in boxer shorts. No easy task as he was still swearing like a trooper and doing his best to resist. Once stripped down to his pants and socks, it was time for a hasty retreat, quickly closing the cell door behind us.

Within minutes of getting into the car, I was sent to another job with helping to track an offender who had stolen several mobile phones in the city centre. Plain clothes officers had been following him, before losing sight of him in the city's back alleys. Jet and I were off again on blue lights, however, it would only take a few minutes for us to get there, being just round the corner from the custody suite.

Jet hopped out the back of the car and struggled to find a scent. Being a busy city centre, even late at night many people had walked through the same area. All we could do was set off in the general direction of the last sighting of the mobile phone thief. We picked up the pace and crisscrossed the city centre, but were unable to locate him. After the high of catching a burglar in the act. This was a low of not being able to locate the thief. However, the mobile phone thief was caught a couple of weeks later with 10 mobile phones stashed down the ladies tights he was wearing.

Sudden Death

Police forces across the UK have paid out a total of £930,000 in compensation to people bitten by police dogs in the past three years. One bite during a chase had led to a pay out of almost £49,000 in another force. That was more than the cost of employing two probationer constables for a year and does nothing to help tight police budgets. Until it is challenged in court, police forces will continue to have to pay out under the current compensation laws/rules. Hopefully at some point government legislation or laws will help reverse this costly aspect of using a police dog to apprehend a suspect or offender.

I had been called in to aid in the search for an attempted burglary on the fringe of the area I used to patrol; three other units were racing to the scene as well, along dark and winding country roads with blue lights flashing. This was the seventh call from the same house reporting of an attempted break-in. Not four hours earlier, a cop had been on the phone to the elderly gentleman who lived there, offering support and advice. We had the furthest to travel and would take the longest to get to the scene. The male that had been reported as trying to break in had been seen jumping off the outhouse roof and then over a wall at the rear of the property.

A local unit was first on scene, followed by the local Sgt. The Sgt had given the local units the exact direction and the location of the property, which was not easy to find, being hidden behind large wooden gates in a small village. The Sgt decided he would search the rear of the house that had a large fence that backed onto a car park and the rear of some other properties. A green wheelie bin lay on its side, which could have been knocked over by the fleeing suspect. It may well be a good place for the dog to begin its search.

Five minutes after the Sgt had arrived, I arrived with Jet. Jet was already barking away with excitement the moment I pulled up, as he knew he was going to be needed. I put Jet on a very long fabric lead and started searching at a wheelie bin, which had been knocked over. Jet picked up a scent immediately and began tracking it back round towards the house where the suspect had last been seen. Jet tracked right back to a fence in the back garden that was on the top of a high wall. There was no way that Jet could go over, so a very eager and young in-service PC Wainwright scrambled up the wall and over the fence. This was followed by the word "FUCK!" a few moments later.

The householder had strategically placed piano wire across the narrow back passage up to his back door and Wainwright had walked straight into it. Thankfully, his stab vest had taken the impact and snapped the wire. It could have lacerated Wainwright's arms or, if it had been a bit higher it would have been his neck. PC Wainwright shouted back that he was OK and then said over the radio that he would give some words of advice to the householder, about the piano wire along his back passage.

I took Jet up and down the street to see if he could pick up another scent but to no avail. PC Wainwright promptly told the householder he expected to see all the piano wire removed in the morning. With the job complete everyone resumed and got back to their patrols. Jet and I, were off to another job - a report of a male who had fled from the scene of an accident. It was on the other side of the city and a good 25 minute drive at speed with blue lights flashing. The male had hit another car before hitting the crash barrier on a dual carriageway. As soon as his badly damaged Corsa had come to a standstill, he had shot off down the road over the crash barrier and into some fields. The helicopter was unavailable due to maintenance and by the time the first local unit made it on scene the job was 15 minutes old. The minute we got to the crash, Jet picked up a scent and began to track. Jet seemed to have a very strong scent straight through a field of knee-high wet grass; Jet was pulling quite strongly in one direction and was already over half a mile from the scene of the crash. Jet kept tracking all the way to the corner of a field that had a drainage ditch and a small group of trees.

As Jet got within five metres of the ditch, he began to bark loudly, so I let him off the lead. Within a few seconds, a bark followed by a yelp could be heard as Jet, bit into the suspect's arm. A very wet and bedraggled male climbed out of the drainage ditch, followed by Jet barking ferociously. I ordered the male to put his hands on his head and handcuffed him to the front initially, before Jet and myself escorted him nearly a mile through the wet and boggy grass to the scene of the crash. Having Jet meant the suspect did not dare make a fuss or any attempt to run off. He knew full well he stood little to no chance of getting away from Jet, and one bite from Jet was enough for him to be totally compliant.

As we got back to our vehicle, local officers were waiting at the scene of the crash to breathalyse the suspect and deal with any other offences. The driver of the other car had escaped injury, but was a little shaken.

After I had retrieved my handcuffs it was time to get back out on patrol and wait for the next call on a busy night it could be almost back-to-back jobs for the entire nine-hour shift.

It was not long before the next call came in, which was to the reports of an elderly gentleman that had not been seen for a few days. With the recent spell of hot weather this could mean a sudden death. With either very cold or very warm weather, sudden deaths involving elderly people do seem to rise. As I was the only available resource and closest I was sent. It was another job Jet would have to sit out, although I think Jet was in a far nicer place - in the boot of the police car. I would get Jet's usual grumble in the form of a bark and a whine, when I did not get him out for a job. Jet always wanted to get out for each and every job we went to.

I walked up to the door and banged heavily on it. I then went round the back and peered through the windows to see if I could see anything. I went back round to the front of the cottage and banged hard on the front door. Still no response. I then opened the letterbox and was just about to shout when this horrible smell of really old rotting garbage hit me. It is an unmistakable smell with a sickly sweetness to it, a smell that you soon learn - is the smell of death. I knew instantly what lay behind the door. I had no choice but to kick the door in. I lifted up my size ten boot and pushed it as hard as I could against the lower part of the door. The door burst open, sending wood splinters flying in every direction as the frame holding the lock gave way with an almighty crack.

As soon as the door opened the very pungent and sickening smell along with the flies could be seen coming from the back of the house. I simply followed the smell that got stronger and stronger as I got closer. As I swung the door to the bedroom open, I could see a body lying in the bed, and it had already started to decompose. The room was full of flies buzzing around. I had to place a tissue over my mouth and nostrils to try and filter out the stench of rotting flesh. The smell made my stomach churn and was the sort of smell that would stick in your nostrils for days.

The smell was so bad, I decided to go outside and get some fresh air whilst I awaited the local doctor and undertaker to arrive in a private ambulance. The undertaker only took 45 minutes to get to me, a new record. Once the doctor had certified time of death, the undertaker moved in to retrieve the body and convey the body to the morgue for an autopsy. It looked as though the old lady had died in her sleep as there was nothing suspicious and no signs of a break-in or foul play. I would spend the last few hours filling in the paperwork for the coroner - a sudden death means the police become an extension of the coroner, looking for potential reasons for the unexpected death. This can include seizing prescription drugs or anything that may be of use to the coroner. I also needed to track down next of kin, for other officers to undertake the sad duty of conveying a death message.

Puppy Love

I first met Jet when he was 12 weeks old, he had just passed the first test to see if he would make a police dog or not due initially to their temperament. I must admit he caught my eye with his cute face and large paws. He was friendly from the outset and almost seemed to have chosen me as opposed to me choosing him first. Puppies are so lovable but also hard work initially and really depend on you almost 24/7. He was kept at the kennels at HQ initially whilst he went through his initial training. Only coming to live with me and my wife when fully trained. But it was a joy to turn up each day to see his cute face and spend eight hours training with him. Watching him grow quite rapidly and soak up the training with such ease. I knew he was going to make a great first police dog, and I am sure has taught me as much as I have taught him over the four years we have been together so far. He is a very determined dog and does not like to give up. He is very friendly at the same time protective of myself and Mrs Blackshaw. He can be a bit over the top when it comes to trying to lick you to death with doggy kisses pouring is love for you out. He especially likes to lick your face, meaning you get a large dose of doggy breath, which is worse after Jet has just eaten.

Jet is a very loving dog and I would not have him any other way; he is a real character. Jet always wants to work and always wants to try to please me. Jet is my son in many ways and my wife, his mother - which is maybe why my wife has not talked about having children since we have had Jet? The downside of getting so close, is you can become too protective. On the odd occasion, it really is hard to let him go to tackle someone wielding a knife as I fear for his safety. I know Jet is a working dog and would rather get stuck in than me hold him back from doing his duty. I still don't know how I would cope if I had to let him tackle an armed assailant. Is a dog's life really worth less than a human? I know some dog lovers would put a dog's life above many not so pleasant human beings.

During training of new police dogs, not all of the puppies make it through some are deemed too shy or do not take to training very well.

These then offered to police officers and staff at the same cost, it has cost us to undertake the basic medical checks and inoculations. The puppies come from a variety of sources, including those donated from the public or bred within the dog unit. Although, those bred from existing police dogs seem to have a natural talent for police work from an early age. Breeding standards are very strict. Dogs are measured against a core set of physical attributes, and are only bred if they meet these criteria.

The key elements needed in a successful police dog are intelligence, aggression, strength, and sense of smell. Most police dogs are male, and are frequently left unneutered so that they maintain their natural aggression. However, this aggression must be kept in check with thorough and rigorous training. Initially, police dogs must first become experts in basic obedience training. They must obey the commands of their handler without hesitation. This is what keeps the inherent aggression of the dog in check, and allows the dog handler to control how much force the dog is using against an offender or suspect. A police dog needs to be comfortable in public places and used to distractions like traffic or large crowds of people such as at a football match or at night in a town centre. The dogs also need to learn basic commands and become responsive to their handlers voice. Each dog is acclimatised to busy city life, because a dog that's nervous around people won't make a good police dog.

With obedience training complete they must also make it through endurance and agility training. The dog must be able to jump over walls and climb stairs.

People often wonder if dogs sniff out hidden drugs because they want to eat them, or because they're addicted to drugs themselves. In fact, the dogs have absolutely no interest in drugs. What they're actually looking for is their favourite toy. Their training has led them to associate that toy with the smell of drugs. Police dogs love to play a vigorous game of tug-of-war with their favourite toy. To begin the training, the handler simply plays with the dog and the toy, which has been carefully washed so that it has no scent of its own. Later, a bag of marijuana is rolled up inside it. After playing for a while, the dog starts to recognize the smell of marijuana as the smell of his favourite toy. The handler then hides the toy, with the drugs, in various places. Whenever the dog sniffs out the drugs, he digs and scratches, trying to get at his toy. He soon comes to learn that if he sniffs out the smell of drugs, as soon as the dog finds them they are rewarded with a ball.

As training progresses, different drugs are placed in the toy, until the dog is able to sniff out a host of illegal substances. The same method is used for bomb-detection dogs, money and cadaver dogs, with the various scents placed inside the toy.

Jet was given scent training for tracking purposes, but a general police dog like Jet does take longer to train and learn all the skills they will need to undertake their role of tracking and apprehending criminals. I also had to go through a tough training course to become a dog handler, before I could begin with helping to train Jet, at the same time bonding with him. Not all dog's and handler get on, some take time to bond and others don't get on at all. It is rare though, as dog handlers are dog lovers themselves and dogs can tell who likes them and who does not. I like to read a dog's eyes as just like humans they are very expressive and a good way to judge a dog's demeanour and character on first contact. This tact is especially useful when I get called out to deal with a dog, be it a stray or one that is being used to guard a cannabis grow or in the house we are about to search. Some of these dogs have been trained to be vicious and I can have a job capturing and containing them. It is a real shame that people train their dogs to be aggressive. Often these dogs end up being put down as they have become dangerous and out of control. Most dogs are not born aggressive some breeds are more aggressive than others. The biggest factor is how they are reared and the type of human interaction they have, that has the biggest impact on a dog's character and overall demeanour.

The first hurdle to becoming a policed dog handler was passing all the entrance criteria for a highly competitive and sought after job. I had to fill out a lengthy application form, along with answering competency based questions that would be marked and scored. Next, I had to attend a formal and quite a gruelling interview. Before finally undertaking a fitness test that was at a higher level than the one undertaken by general police officers. Once I made it through that I was then off to undertake my dog handling course. This was an intensive course and covered everything from actual dog handling to welfare and dog first aid. Even though I thought I knew quite a bit about dogs - the training showed how much I did not know. In total it lasted 12 weeks. The first 8 weeks were at a police dog training centre followed by a four week course on operational skills back at my force HQ. Even with training complete, both Jet and I have to attend a 10 day refresher course once a year to ensure my handling skills are up to scratch and Jet is performing as he should. This and the constant daily grooming and health check I have to undertake on Jet, all go on behind the scenes far from public view and the many police documentaries splashed across our screen. The grooming alone involves using your hands to massage the dog's coat as this stimulates circulation within the dog's skin. Then use a brush to firstly brush the coat following the direction of the hair and then against the direction of the hair. The final step is to use a comb to ensure all dead skin and hair has been removed.

Whilst being a highly enjoyable and rewarding job, being a dog handler can also be a demanding one. But a job I would not change for anything else, I get to do two things I love, dogs and police, whilst getting paid for the privilege. There is the odd day I have to pinch myself to think it is not a dream. Just as I have the odd day thinking I am quite mad to do what I do, working all hours of the day and night, whilst enduring physical and verbal abuse.

Car Thieves

Operational dogs often experienced failure. A track could lead to nowhere, a search would find nothing, an offender being pursued would escape and no matter how much the handler tried to compensate with fun exercises. Jet seemed to take each one these failures personally. Success was at the core of being the best dog and handler within the force we always liked to get our 'man.' There are however some guarantees, like an offender who runs into a building and then head for the toilets thinking hiding behind a cubicle door in the toilet will somehow make them invisible. With the thought of locking themselves in and standing on the seat or maybe climbing out through a small window. This was a reality and sometimes having offenders who are not the brightest crayons in the packet gave Jet the edge and we would come out victorious. More from the offender's stupidity than Jet's ability to track, but of course Jet would need to pick up the scent and I would guide him towards the toilets.

Two estates in the north of the county originally separated, but are now joined together with a new housing development. Have gradually become the residential area of choice for those that were better off. Modern 4 and 5 bedroom luxury homes with large gardens, built in the last six years, sandwiched between a 1960s and 1970s council housing. Parked on the drives of these luxury homes were new BMWs, Range Rovers, Audis and even the odd Aston Martin and Bentley. These sort of homes, sadly attracted burglars from the less affluent areas of the city. By the day they would drive in what can best be described as a normal Ford or Vauxhall hatchback and break into houses, especially those that had left a window open to make for easy entry. At night the burglaries could become more sinister with gangs of mainly eastern Europeans and usually part of Organised Crime Groups, breaking in to steal car keys in order to steal the prestige cars sitting on the drive. These cars would then either be shipped abroad, or dismantled and again the parts shipped abroad in shipping containers. If challenged they would and have turned violent their prize and its financial worth having a greater worth than human life.

The day burglars generally liked to steal electrical items such as TVs, Xboxes, PS4s and so on along with Jewellery, which was easy to hide on their person and easy to sell on. If they were spotted or the area became too hot due to a strong police presence after burglary their favourite place to hide their haul was in a wheelie bin and then come back later to collect it. On one sunny morning for whatever reason the burglars decided to change what they stole and instead went for a brand new Audi Q5 4x4 after the keys had been left lying on the kitchen table and the back door unlocked. It was an obvious temptation which was too hard for them to resist. The downside was, that with someone at home and the noise a car would make, it would soon alert them to the fact their car had been stolen and only give the burglars a limited getaway time before the area was flooded with police cars. Burglary was a high priority at the moment and any burglary with offenders on scene or a burglary in progress meant as many resources in terms of police officers were told to go to the area and put a cordon in place. It had resulted in some good results, although many burglars were still able to make good their escape. However, stealing a car in daylight was going to be difficult, as there were not many roads in and out of the area, although a fast 60mph A road connected all the estates together and fed into the ring road. It was the perfect day for flying. If available the police helicopter could lift and be in the area within 10 minutes. Sure enough the burglars were seen stealing the vehicle by a neighbour, then heard driving off by the householder. Police were quickly alerted and local units along with a traffic car were sent to the area.

 Not long after, I was also requested just in case the burglars decided to stop, before trying and run from the car and Jets tracking talents were required. The helicopter was currently at another job, but would race to the area the moment it had finished. Along with the rest of the police officers we all raced to the area, luck was our side that day as a local officer spotted the Q5, three up travelling along an A road and tried to follow at speed. The burglars sped up and we now had a full blown pursuit. The traffic car finally made it to the area and took the lead, I also was not too far away if the car was dumped. The speed of the pursuit rose and top desk as it is known, or the control room Inspector monitored carefully and had to make the decision to continue or not. As it was early afternoon on a dry sunny day, it was not too dangerous at this time. Desperate people will do desperate things to get away, this usually means putting the general public at risk. If the police causes an accident in the process, it tends to ruffle allot of feathers, especially the media, who currently in some circles don't seem to like the police very much.

The burglars were not the best drivers and as the speed rose seemed to be having a greater difficulty controlling the car. Weaving all over the road after a corner or roundabout as they entered and exited with too much speed. The pursuit was now 10 minutes old the helicopter was on route racing to the scene at 145 mph. The Q5 was swerving around moving vehicles at 80 to 90 mph, overtaking on blind bends and everything that usually would add up to a crash, hopefully not involving an innocent driver. As the Q5 rounded a corner and started its way up the hill the car just ran off the road and ended up on its side in the ditch, the traffic car was close behind and in the initial confusion it had been thought the driver had made off across the field towards a wood. The helicopter was still making its way out to us, so I would be first on scene to start tracking the driver, I awaited further updates from the scene as the traffic car realised the car had not been three up but potentially four up. Two were taken out of the wrecked car with still one passenger remaining partially trapped. His leg had become trapped underneath. The Fire Service had been called to attend the scene to remove the trapped male. Smoke was starting to pour out the car and the high risk of fire, by now I was in the midst of four other police cars at the scene, other officers had quickly closed off. I got Jet out the back of the car who as usual was eager to get stuck in and begin tracking, just as we were about to start. I heard a shout from one of the traffic officers, "There is no runner mate, we have identified that we already have the driver and the car was three up. I don't suppose you have a spare fire extinguisher do you? We have used one and the vehicle has started to burn and set alight to the hedge it is now propped up against." I said "No probs," hoping Fire would be here pretty soon. Car fires can take hold very quickly and it never ceases to amaze me the speed in which fire can spread. The biggest concern was that we had a person trapped in the car and if the fire took hold, we would struggle to save him.

I remember going out to reports of an RTC (Road Traffic Collision) involving two teenagers who had managed to drive the car off road and down an embankment, the car had quickly caught fire and when I arrived it was fully alight. The most painful and disturbing element, was hearing those two teenagers screams as they burnt to death. Unable to do anything as the heat was too intense for me to even get close to the fully alight car. Those screams remain with me and is still the most harrowing and heart breaking job I have been too. The families were never told that their sons had died in agony, to save them the extra pain. But, I have never felt so helpless and unable to do anything, even though I was a fully trained police officer. My single fire extinguisher would have not stood even a slight chance against a car fully ablaze. Not that I would have been able to have got close enough to be able to use it. It is a good example of what can happen if two young people decided to drive in a dangerous manner, paying the ultimate price for their spirited driving.

Just as I got Jet back into the car, Fire turned up and quickly got stuck into putting the fire out and checking he casualty, whilst an Ambulance was still on route. The Fire Service and Ambulance are another amazing group of people who also work in difficult conditions and situations to save lives. Sadly, these days, we often get called out to protect them from rowdy teenagers or someone that requires help but does not want it and turns violent.

Fire, took minutes to put the fire out before turning their attentions to getting the casualty out. Their plan was to use airbags to lift the car up just enough to be able to pull the male passenger free. The other two occupants were already on their way to custody and the police helicopter was buzzing overhead taking pictures of the crash scene which would form part of the investigation. As the crash involved a pursuit by police vehicles it would also need to be investigated by the Independent Police Complaints Commission (IPCC) oversees the police complaints system in England and Wales and sets the standards by which the police should handle complaints. It is independent, making its decisions entirely independently of the police and government. Usually high speed pursuits resulting in a crash, death in custody, all police firearms discharges or where the mishandling of a situation has led to a mistake or mistakes in an investigation. I do agree that the police need an independent body to avoid cover ups which have occurred in the past. As police we do need to be held accountable for our actions. At the same time, police officers often have to make dynamic decisions in the heat of the moment, which at the time was the best and most appropriate option. With hindsight, there maybe was a better way forward but that extra time needed is not always available to a police officer in a very dynamic situation. This needs to also be taken into account. As humans, we do and will make mistakes. Not always intentional, but when seconds count instinct and training usually takes precedent, especially with the adrenaline flowing. Sitting down in a quiet room would probably mean you would make a very different decision having the time to fully think through the consequences.

As professionals, we do have monthly training days to keep up to date with changes in the law and procedure. Along with better ways to improve our interactions with the public. I would like to think I am always respectful and courteous to everyone. Although sometimes it is hard at the end of a busy nine hour shift feeling tired and stressed to remain composed, with someone quite unpleasant.

The Fire Brigade took around an hour to free the male from the Q5 - straight into the arms of the awaiting ambulance crew. He had been lucky and escaped with a fractured leg and a few cuts and bruises. All three were later charged with burglary and vehicle theft. They all ended up with custodial sentences. It also had the desired effect of reducing burglaries in the area for around six months before they started up again. Often a spate of burglaries is conducted by the same person or persons, we either lock them up or they go to another area, and burglaries either stopped or are vastly reduced. During the interview, they are always asked if they would like to 'cough' up to any other burglaries. Thus helping detection rates and also giving the victim some piece of mind that the burglar ad been caught.

Day Off

Days off are not as exciting as rushing around at Mach 10 with your hair on fire or blue lights flashing. Stealing a line form one of my favourite films 'Top Gun,' not sure if it is the flying or the music but have always loved it since watching it on TV. My usual shift pattern is six days on and four days off. The first two days are spent on a day shift usually 7 until 4, but if a raid was planned, I could start at 4 or 5 am. After two days on day shift, you switch to afternoon or 'afters' 3 until 12 am, finally comes two days of nights, 10 until 7 am. After a night shift it is home to bed for a few hours, although Jet usually manages to get some sleep in between jobs on nights his snoring often being quite audible. Jet can be quite vocal when he is asleep growling or twitching of his paws as if he is trying to catch something. I would love to know what dogs dream about. Judging by Jet they must dream like we do, just I would imagine their dreams are about doggy things?

On most nights, things tend to calm down by around 2 or 3am and I either head back for paperwork or patrol a particular area that is currently a high priority area.

After a few hours' sleep on my first rest day and having the house to myself, if it is a weekday – the wife being at work. I tend to take Jet out for a long work and bonding session, sometimes it is out into the countryside, other times it is through the local park. Jet is quite a bounder when he is let off his lead. He is disciplined and highly trained, but you can see the looks of horror on other dog owners face's as he comes pelting over towards them and their much smaller breed of dog. Jet loves going for long walks and to be honest, I enjoy it too. Jet makes for excellent company and I can look quite mad as I chat away to him, putting the world to rights. Sometimes Jet comes on a cross country run with me only in the warmer and drier weather though, due to Jet not liking a bath. Although too many baths washes the oils away that protect his coat and can also dry his skin out.

Usually after our long walk we head to a local burger van and both have a bacon roll, before heading back home. Ready for me to give Jet his daily groom and health check. Then I have another snooze on the sofa catching up with some sleep, with Jet either beside me squashing me or at my feet. Being a dog handler really is a lifestyle – much more so than a police officer. I suppose I really do take my work home with me, but that work is a real pleasure. If I do want a holiday abroad then Jet is put in the kennels at the force HQ. I do miss him though, even if it is nice to have a break from the daily grind. Jet is part of the family and even though she tries to hide it my wife loves him just as much as I do. He is also very protective of her. Once I was across the road popping into a shop and Jet was standing next to Mrs Blackshaw. An old school friend of Mrs Balckshaw approached her and tried to give her a hug. Jet bit him in the leg in the process, thinking he was up to something more sinister. Thankfully, the male saw the funny side, even though my wife was mortified and very apologetic. By way of compensation he requested that I took him for a tour of the dog section as he was really interested. He currently had an application in to join the British Transport Police. It could have ended much worse with an official complaint and compensation being paid out.

  Jet will be a very good dog as and when we decide to have children. I can see Jet being very protective and almost standing on guard duty. I am sure there will be some jealousy as well. Jet gets jealous now if my wife snuggles up to me on the sofa or I give her a kiss that is a bit too long. Acting like a chaperone, Jet will try to snuggle in between us or just offer up a few licks to ensure he does not go unnoticed.

  As a pup he used to sleep on the sofa with us and I was tempted to initially let him sleep on the bed, but was warned about bad habits and did I really want a fully grown German Shepherd in the bed for the next 10 years. Even though it is hard to listen to their pines for the first couple of nights as they settle into their bedtime routine. Jet now lives in his own large kennel in the garden which my police force paid for along with all his food, vet ills and yearly inoculations. Jet if you like, is an employee just like myself so his pay comes in the form of a nice kennel and dog food, along with free medical care.

  As for me, well, I just ensure I always follow BOND, and not the famous secret agent of the silver screen either…

B – Believing in the dog is of prime importance. Many operational cases and experiences illustrate this point. If the handler has the tendency to lead the dog while tracking they will never become a proficient team since the dog will soon become discouraged and refuse to work properly. It is the duty of every dog handler to follow their dog and investigate indications made by the dog no matter how impossible it may seem. By believing in the dog greater success and appreciation will follow. It is not intended that the handler should follow blindly behind the dog. It must be remembered that dog handling is a team effort as such; the handler must be mentally alert and assist the dog when necessary. However, he should not doubt the ability of his charge.

O – Observe the Dog – Each dog must be treated with individual consideration. This is because each dog communicates or indicates through actions, in a different manner. The dog handler must be observant in order to interpret the actions of the dog. If the dog handler is not mentally alert they may miss the indication of their dog or they may misinterpret an indication. This could mean the difference between success and failure.

N – Nurture This word not only pertains to diet, but also the education or teaching of the dog. Some people feel that there is no limit to what a dog can be taught. With the use of imaginative training and hard work, a dog possessing the necessary core abilities will become increasingly effective. Its handler must contribute as much as possible to the education of their charge. By simulating actual working conditions the dog will become very proficient and confident. The more time the handler spends with the dog the closer the union will become between the two.

D – Depend on one another – The dog will learn to depend on its handler and must respect the handler as its master. The handler will care for the dog in all respects. It is the duty of the handler to care for the dog in the best possible way. On the other hand, the handler must depend on the dog, hence a mutual feeling of dependence. The dog is the handler's so called 'working partner'. If the handler has followed all the instruction and tuition received, applied the knowledge on to their dog through training and completed their responsibilities to the dog's welfare and well-being, then the handler should have a proficient helper on whom they can depend.

Tracking

After some disorder in a local town centre I was asked to go along with Jet as a further visible presence to cool things down a bit. A large fight involving about 25 people had broken out and 15 had been arrested for affray. However, tensions were still running high and it is amazing how just having a police dog in the vicinity helps to quell things, as very few want to mess with a police dog. The odd drunk that, 'tries to have a go' usually gets a growl or a bark from Jet if they get too close and quickly make a hasty retreat. Tonight it was a case of patrolling around the streets with Jet for a couple of hours, which was very pleasant being the end of a hot sunny day. Jet did what he needed to do which was calm the situation down and help get people off home rather than arguing in the street.

The rest of the night was pretty much uneventful, until it was 6:30am and I was just about to head back to HQ for the end of the shift when I got a call of a burglary at a posh mansion out in the country side. The details were sketchy as to whether the burglary was in progress or had just been found. On arrival, an old woman, who said she had just been burgled, greeted me. The house looked pristine, I wondered what she was talking about. She took me to the safe in the bedroom, saying,

"Right this way, young man." Once inside, she showed me about £250,000 worth of jewellery; diamonds, rubies, gold, even a signed invitation to the Queen's tea party.

She then ordered me to take it all away as it was fake. She continued to say that the robbers took all her real stuff and substituted it for this fake jewellery, and that she wanted it all getting rid of. I agreed to placate her, but knew something was not quite right with her. I asked if she had any family who could come and help them take it all away, as it was too much for me to carry.

She promptly passed the number for her son. He explained to me in a sleepy voice over the phone that, since her husband had died, she just kept slipping away and the dementia was getting worse. They had tried to get her into a home, but she had flatly refused. With that, I said to the old woman that they would come back to collect everything later, but for now we would keep it in her safe. I went and locked the safe before checking the rest of the house was secure, before making sure the elderly woman was back in bed and left, locking the door behind me. I was then finally able to get off duty an hour late.

After this night shift it was time for four days off before back for an extra early start to help in the search or a missing person. The missing person was now believed to have been murdered. Mark and his Springer Spaniel Bono could also assist in the search as drugs had been thought to have been involved in the murder, and possibly fining drugs, may lead to more evidence or even finding a body.

We had a 5am start in order to get to a briefing for the search we were going to undertake for a Latvian male who had initially been reported missing by his mother in Latvia and the evidence to the flat had led to the belief that he had been murdered. Our job was to search for a body, normally a cadaver dog is the best option, but we don't currently have one and usually borrow a dog from another force. However, this dog was unavailable and Jet was seen as the next best thing.

The briefing lasted about half an hour and covered the area that we would be expected to search, which was an area of scrub land about a mile from the victim's home. The suspects had been interviewed several times, but had not revealed anything. The area we were searching was very much a "best guess." Jet would search in short shifts as his nose would become less effective and fatigued if he was trying to find the victims smell. Any potential track would be long gone and we were looking for a body. A cadaver dog is trained to be able to search for a body that has been buried as searches for the smell of a decomposing corpse. It will then give an active response, as police dogs can be trained to give an active or passive response.

When a police dog finds what he's sniffing for he lets his handler know it's there by giving the alert signal. Drug dogs use an aggressive alert - they dig and paw at the spot where they smell the drugs, trying to get at the toy they think is waiting there. However, there are some specialties where an aggressive alert would not be a good idea. If a dog searching for a bomb digs and scratches at it when he finds it, the results could be disastrous. In these cases, a passive alert is used and the dog may indicate by sitting down.

I got Jet out of the car and put him on the long fabric lead to begin trying to pick up a scent. Jet was slow to learn tracking and he was behind the other dogs when it came to going on an extended leash. I must partially take the blame as being a new handler I was also on a steep learning curve. As a dog improves at tracking the tracking line is replaced with an extended leash. The tracking line is not just the means of keeping in contact with the dog whilst it is working - it is a line of communication which, if properly used will make the handler sensitive to the dog's movements and indications. As a handler you must appreciate that the standard of the line handling has a strong influence on the efficiency eventually reached by the dog. At the start of a track, when the tracking line has been taken into use, you carefully lay the line out on the ground to its full extent ensuring that it is free from knots and not tangled. After attaching the line to the harness on the dog, the leash is removed. As the dog is set to work, you gradually allow the line to pass through your hand until an appropriate distance between handler and dog has been reached. Over time the dog becomes more and more adept at this to the point where it becomes almost instinctive for both the dog and the handler.

As per usual Jet was excited to be working and you could see the glee in his eyes as we made our way across the first small area in small woodland just off the scrub land. The woodland would be an ideal area to hide a body, but may be too much Midsomer Murders for us to actually find a body there. After an hour's search we had come up empty handed and it was time for a quick play with the ball as a reward for Jet's efforts. The day pretty much was, search an area for an hour stop, then search another area. Sadly, all the searching, we undertook we came up with nothing. This meant it would be back to the drawing board for the major incident team from CID. Feeling very tired after only a few hours' sleep, I was more than happy to get off duty and return home to catch up with some much needed sleep. Jet also seemed tired; I had to virtually drag him out the car when I got home.

***

After my days off, with two days falling over the weekend, meant I got to spend some time with my wife and have a lovely picnic at a local country park. Jet got a bowl of cut up cooked chicken. I do have to be careful with Jet's diet though, and ensure he is fed correctly to keep him healthy.

After my four rest days, I was back on duty, back on days, and not long into my shift when I got called to reports of a male who was high on drink and drugs strolling down the street clutching a 13-inch knife he had just used.

The male was a known drug addict called Chris Halbert. He had just stabbed his girlfriend, a mother of one, multiple times in the chest in a frenzied attack at their home. He then threw a duvet over the 22-year-old as she lay dying, and walked out holding the murder weapon, saying he had left her for dead according to witnesses on the street

He had been due in court the day before to hear charges of assault and drug possession. However, he had failed to appear and a warrant for his arrest had only just been circulated. With a direction of travel and with CCTV following him, Myslef and Jet raced to the area. Initially, Chris could not be found, but one witness suggested trying his brother's house. I was first on scene and got out with Jet and banged loudly on the front door. Chris's brother came to the door and I noticed blood on one of his hands. I then pushed the brother aside and went inside to search the house. As I was unsure that Chris was in the house at that time, I assumed Chris's brother had the knife.

I found Chris upstairs hiding under a duvet covered in blood.

Chris kept saying, "She's dead, she's dead, no one is going to have her now."

Local police in the area soon located the discarded knife in a front garden not too far from Chris's home address. Within 45 minutes of the call, we had managed to apprehend the offender and recover the murder weapon; a good result in tragic circumstances. Two Armed response guys finally joined me and quickly arrested Chris and took him to the custody suite.

Within a minute of getting back into the police car, I got the next call to a suicide attempt. The caller had allegedly taken an intentional overdose of prescription medication in an attempt to kill himself. Despite the fact that he called the police the subject told control that he did not want the police to respond. He added that he had barricaded himself in his bedroom.

While en route to the call control said the subject sounded like he may be losing consciousness. Control maintained contact with the caller for as long as possible. They advised that the caller had been known to carry a weapon. Upon arrival, two other officers met me a few houses from the male's residence to formulate a plan. I got control to call the male again, but they received no answer. As they began walking toward the house. They saw a vehicle parked in the driveway and a young couple with a baby entering the house. Fearing that the couple had unknowingly placed themselves and their baby in danger, they decided to enter the house to evacuate them and attempt to contact the suicidal male.

Once inside the house, they located the couple and their baby and directed them outside. The couple explained to me that they had rented a room inside the residence as had the suicidal male. They mentioned that there were likely to be other people in the residence, but were unable to confirm whether anyone else was home because all the flat doors were locked. The couple pointed out the suicidal male's window and they all made their way upstairs to contact him.

I tried to talk to the suicidal male, "Hey mate, it is the police. We just want to talk to you. Open the door, we need to make sure you're alright."

The man did not reply and just started to grunt.

I tried negotiating with the male to open the door for several minutes. He became more hostile as he swore, yelled and became more hysterical. One of the Armed Response guys kicked in the flimsy bedroom door with an enforcer or 'big red key' as it is also known.

Upon impact, the door was literally ripped in half, and the enforcer penetrated a wooden dresser that the male had propped against the door. As soon as the door was open, I backed away from the doorway and drew my Taser as the other officers pointed their Tasers at the subject.

The man was standing in an aggressive stance near the front door holding a large fixed-blade knife in his left hand. I could not see his right hand because he kept it behind the dresser that had been used to barricade the door.

I continued to point my Taser at the subject as John and the other two Armed Response officers provided extra Taser cover, ready to engage if needed.

I said, "DROP THE KNIFE or I will use the Taser. DROP THE KNIFE."

When the male disobeyed all verbal commands to drop the knife I fired my Taser causing both probes to imbed in the man's chest area. The man fell to the floor immobile and one of the armed response guys rushed in to handcuff him without further incident. The Taser works by small nitrogen charges propelling two long wires with barbs on the end, these barbs are basically hooks, which can penetrate light clothing and attach themselves to the skin. A high voltage charge is then released which incapacitates an individual.

Once back in custody, the suicidal male thanked me for using my Taser to subdue him. He mentioned that had it not been for the police he would have killed himself that day. He was assessed before being given a psychiatric assessment and admitted to hospital for mental health problems. After that incident the rest of the shift was pretty uneventful. That is the nature of police work, racing from job to job or driving around waiting for a call to come in for hours on end.

Fish Pond

One night, whilst I was on patrol standing in for response, which was short staffed that night. Jet had so far spent most of the shift cooped up in the back of the car. I was asked to go and see an old woman who was in a distressed condition. On arrival at her house I was informed by a relative that she had been unable to contact her sister and was concerned about her welfare. She lived in a block of flats about two miles away. It took only a few minutes for me to reach the flats and as I arrived, I found that I was unable to park nearby. This meant I had to park further away and cut across a grassed area around the back of the flats. Half wishing I had brought Jet with me for extra protection. As I ambled across the grass I noticed a strange flickering light coming from the window of a ground floor flat with faint wisps of smoke emanating from inside. On closer inspection, I saw a yellow glow and hot window that obviously signalled a fire.

I ran around to the communal entrance door and having already got on the radio to control to alert the fire brigade. I checked with a neighbour and realised that an elderly lady lived here. With no sign of the fire service, I took the decision, possibly a foolish decision to put the door in and took an almighty kick. Putting my hip out in the process. Several seconds passed before my hip slipped slowly back into its socket; the door hadn't moved an inch. I continued kicking at the door, finding strength that only comes when adrenaline starts to pump, and I finally kicked in the door and frame quickly followed by some bricks and plaster.

The door had in fact stayed locked shut with numerous locks and it was the frame that had failed. Edging along the hallway, keeping low I was able to shut the door to the living room where the fire had taken complete hold. Flames were seeping out of the living room door and along the hall ceiling. It was obvious that there would have been no hope for anyone who was still remaining in the living room. On investigating the rest of the flat. I opened a bedroom door to find a surreal image. Sat up in bed, false teeth in a glass at her side with smoke swirling around her, was an old lady reading a book. Realising that I was there and not recognising me as a police officer, she screamed at me to get out. If I had forced her out, I would have most probably given her a heart attack. So I dashed back out of the flat and ran back in shouting

"POLICE! Anyone there?"

"Yes," said a soft croaky voice.

This time, the old lady decided I was indeed a police officer and agreed to make her way out of the flat with me, once she had put her teeth back in.

The other old lady, who I had originally been sent to see was safe and well. She was evacuated by the fire brigade who had now turned up to the fire. I got a commendation for my actions, even though I don't feel I actually did anything heroic. I was even told I should have stayed back until the fire brigade had arrived. It was one of those situations where you do not think, but act on instinct, especially when another life is in mortal danger.

That was the first of the two slightly strange jobs I would attend that night. After being checked over by the ambulance crew for smoke inhalation, I put myself back on duty known as 'state 2' or on patrol. As I knew how stretched resources were that night. An hour later, I got called to a person suffering mental illness. The individual Zain had come into contact with the police on numerous other occasions. I was told by control that Zain could at times be very unpredictable and difficult to handle. He had turned up in an affluent area, and I had received a radio message to the effect that a 6 foot 2 inch black male had just abandoned a car, stolen a piece of clothing off a washing line and made well his escape. I already knew it was Zain due to another officer coming over the Airwave radio system to tell me it was most likely Zain, due to the description given. Because of the markers against him for violence Armed Response were also travelling and they had already been given Taser authority. I quickly found the car which had been reported stolen, but I could see no sign of the person responsible for stealing and then abandoning it. A search of the area was made with a negative result even with Jet helping me to track him.

Within half an hour, another report came in of a 6 foot 2 inch black male talking to fish in a garden pond. I arrived at the scene to find that the description matched Zain and the male at the fish pond. The male was indeed engaged in a serious conversation with several goldfish.

This was a situation where experience was really going to be needed. By now, an Armed Response officer had joined me and Jet. I approached the man, ensuring that the pond was between myself and the male at all times, keeping Jet on a very short leash. But the Armed Response officer decided to try and talk to the man face-to-face. I tried to warn him, but it was too late; the man had the Armed Response officer in the pond and was holding him underwater with arms locked at full stretch. This male was clearly very powerful. I looked around for help but the householder, who had been an interested spectator up until that point, had suddenly decided that it was time to make a rapid exit. This was getting serious; if I jumped in the pond to help, we could all end up dead and Jet would also most likely make the situation worse by trying to protect me. I managed to reach across, grab the man's quite wild hair and pull him towards the side of the pond. Jet was now starting to bark and had become quite excited.

I then, contrary to all policies and procedures, hit the man as hard as he could several times right in the middle of the head with my ASP. I also carried a Taser, but electricity and water do not mix and would have most likely ended shocking the armed response officer. The head is classed as a red area, i.e. one that you do not hit unless in a life threatening situation which I classed this one to be. The man released the Armed Response officer who popped up from under the water like a bright red cork. The man then turned on me, asking "What's with the pain, man?" before stepping from the pond and making his way towards me. He was closely followed by the Armed Response guy who, considering the circumstances, was making a remarkable recovery. My hair stood on end as I thought I was in for a right good pummelling and drew my Taser. Putting the red dot squarely on the man's chest. I was also going to release Jet after I had Tasered the man, just in case he kept coming such was my fear of this male who seemed more cyborg than human.

I honestly thought he was going to be killed or seriously injured. Then for no apparent reason, the man stopped as if in a trance. I took the opportunity and handcuffed Zain within seconds before he became absolutely wild and was Tasered by the dripping wet, Armed Response officer. It was amazing after being dunked that his Taser still worked. Zain was taken to a mental health unit and sedated. A later examination found that he had suffered no injuries as a result of my action which caused allot of extra paperwork. I was relieved to not have suffered any injury to myself.

I was back at work at 11am the next morning after just a few hours' sleep due to a search warrant that had been arranged. For a cannabis factory on a quiet urban street in a more affluent area of the city. Normally we should have at least 12 hours between shifts, but duties had been changed after no other dog was available for the warrant. The Operational Support Group had also been called in for the drugs raid. OSG got themselves kitted up in riot gear whilst the Sgt running the raid went to collect the warrant from the magistrate's court.

Once the Sgt was back with the warrant, everyone was able to climb aboard two Mercedes Sprinter vans before making their way to the house to execute the warrant. On arrival, OSG made sure the back and the front of the house were covered, before using the enforcer to break down the front door. As the OSG officers piled through the front door, a male in cutoff tracksuit bottoms and a t-shirt tried to make good his escape through the back door, and ran straight into the path of myself and Jet covering the rear. He was quickly cuffed to the front and I took him back inside. On the ground floor, OSG came to a locked door that they assumed might lead to what should have been the living room. After breaking down the living room door, they found that it was full of mature cannabis plants with a street value of about £30,000. The room had all the hydroponics equipment and the heating system for the plants, which had been hard-wired directly into the mains, bypassing the meter. Some of the plants would be sent to the lab to be tested to 'confirm' they were cannabis plants, although the distinctive and the overpowering smell emanating from the room made it obvious they were cannabis plants. Nevertheless, they would still need to be tested for evidential reasons. It took nearly an hour to bag all the plants up before they were taken back to the property store at the local police station. A couple of the plants were then sent to the lab for testing, and the rest would later be destroyed.

It had been a satisfying raid, with another cannabis factory closed down and an arrest made. Other cannabis farms would almost certainly pop elsewhere, almost as soon as one was taken down. Last year he police raided 7000 grows nationally and more and more are popping up each week. Myself and OSG went back to the police station to sort out the paperwork and get everything seized, put into the property safe and booked in, although other than an arrest statement, I was able to escape the majority of the paperwork and booking exhibits into the property store.

Just as I was about to leave a job came in of a van driver who had been stopped by some local officers just down the road. I had been asked to go and assist at the request of the local officers. The van, when checked, came up as having a drugs marker and the cops carried out a routine search of the car for drugs. A man stepped out with a small dog under his arm and was fully compliant. As one of the officers searched the male, a needle was found, along with some other needles in the back of his van.

Further searching revealed some suspicious packages that the male protested were harmless. As the officers searching the car believed they were drugs, the male was promptly arrested for possession of a class A drug. As for the poor dog, it would end up in the police kennels until its owner was released and able to come and collect it. I got the job of collecting the job and putting it in the empty cage next to Jet, in the back of the car, much to Jet's disgust of having a very yappy small dog next to him. It was not for long, before I had the dog in the kennels of a local police station, ready to be collected either by the offender or the dog warden if the offender did not get released. I felt sorry for the poor little thing, she did look scared and bemused by what was happening to her.

    The biggest mistake dog owners can make with their dogs is to treat them like humans. The human race overall is a kind, compassionate species that we tend to look at our canine companions as little humans, when in reality, they are canines and have a very different thought process. This is what differentiates mankind from other species in pack societies; there must be a specific order, from the leader on down to the last follower. Everyone has a place. The leaders are the strength of the pack, while the followers need the leader to guide them. Dogs have an instinct to constantly test the being above them and an instinct to know they will always be tested by the being below them. Instinct tells them that if there is not a strong being in charge, their life and the lives of the rest of their pack are at stake. This primal instinct keeps the pack secure and happy. That is why dogs must have a master and without one they do feel lost.

    Dogs instinctively crave rules to follow and limits as to what they are allowed to do. When dogs live with humans, the humans become the dog's pack. For the relationship to succeed, humans must become the dog's pack leader. The mistake is made when the humans in the pack only give the dog love and overlook the other needs of a dog. To a dog, constant affection without rules and limits goes against every grain in its instinct. While dogs enjoy being given affection, it does not satisfy the animal and it is not what makes them well balanced, stable minded, secure and happy. Dogs love affection, however, that alone does not make a dog happy, satisfying its instincts do. You need to provide proper emotional stability in order to achieve this, and showing you have an orderly pack with rules to follow is what the dog needs. Giving your dog affection is important for the human, and enjoyed by the dog, but must be done at the correct times.

    A dog is an animal and does not possess the same reasoning skills as a human. Dogs do have emotions, but their emotions are different than those of humans. They are simple creatures with instincts, and their emotions, lack a complex thought process. They feel joy when they know you are pleased, they feel sad when someone dies. However, they do not premeditate or plan ahead, and do not dwell in the past or future. They live for whatever is happening at the moment.

Lost Boy

I had been called to help out at a job supporting some other police officers looking for what had been classed as a high risk missing person. A man heavily in drink had been involved in a domestic incident with his wife and during the process had hit his wife several times. Even though there was a concern for his safety he was also wanted for the assault on his wife.

I knew the country park quite well after having taken Jet there on a regular basis. I went in one entrance with Jet and told the other police officers to enter via the side entrance. A path leading into the country park ran at the back of the house where the domestic had taken place. The police helicopter arrived overhead to do a wider area search; this was quite an extensive country park with many small tree copses, a lake and areas you could easily go to ground in if so desired. The park also had a heritage railway within it which gave another area which was easy to hide in and needed to be searched.

After the helicopter had not found anything. Despite doing a wide search of the entire park. I said that we would check the railway station and rolling stock. A PCSO at the same time would also be able to re-kindle his childhood love of trains even if it was in the pitch black dark. Walking along an empty section of railway line the PCSO went and tripped over a railway sleeper. Just missing a very oily locomotive bogie which would have given him a lovely oil stain on his uniform. I was in stitches as I saw the PCSO stumble - I suppose my dark sense of humour. I found that these old locomotives had a really strong stench of oil and diesel that stayed up his nose for an hour or two. To me, these old relics should be scrapped there was nothing heritage about them. They were just plain smelly and dirty. I was worried about Jet getting sticky black oil on his lovely coat.

We searched the entire station area and all the rolling stock and this proved negative. They then also decided to search the local roads around the park and that came up negative as well. At this point, everyone was stood down and it was hoped the male would turn up at some point. Patrols would continue to keep a close eye on the park overnight and then another search would be conducted in daylight. The male was found the next morning camping out in a wooded area of the park which had been searched by the helicopter and cops. In the dark, he had not been seen. The helicopter with its thermal imaging camera had a chance of picking him out, but even the helicopter and its thermal cameras had been unable to spot him. It was probable that in the wooded area he had erected his tent and unintentionally shielded his thermal image from even the helicopter.

Heading back along the main road to HQ, I came up behind a Vauxhall Astra that was weaving slightly. My immediate thought was, "drink driver." When safe to do so I pulled the car over and a petite lady who was struggling to walk on very high heeled platform shoes got out of the car. I cannot begin to imagine how she could possibly drive a car in those shoes. My instinct clicked in and I knew the chances of her blowing over the limit were very high indeed. Sure enough, she blew 45 and was promptly arrested and taken to custody. It was 1:50am and I had been due to get off at 2am which was not going to happen now.

I had some empathy with the woman as she explained she had been due to stay at her friend's house. They had fallen out during the evening and she was now stranded with no way of getting home. However, she did admit that she could have got her boyfriend to pick her up, but did not want to hassle him. She had not been drinking that heavily and it had been a couple of hours since her last drink. She still realised that she should not have been driving though. For that bad decision it was hard to have any sympathy really.

In custody, I did the formal breath test on the intoxyliser, which proved her to be over the limit. She then also opted for a blood test. The blood test would take a little longer as it meant I had to wait for a nurse to come and administer it. With the wait, I got on with the paperwork and the all-important arrest statement. After the blood test, I offered to take the lady back to her car as it was now just after 5am and she would probably be below the limit. Before letting her get behind the wheel I did another quick breath test to check. Sure enough, she was below the limit so could at least safely drive home. It was much safer to do this than expecting her to find a taxi or walk even a short distance in the early hours of the morning. The blood results came back a week later and she was still over the limit, later receiving a 12 month driving ban at court.

Parade

There are times, when Jet does not always do quite as he should. We had been invited to attend the Lord Mayors parade with a variety of other dignitaries. I was dressed in my court or dress uniform of a tunic and formal trousers along with the traditional Custodian helmet worn by male police officers. We were lined up and the Mayor had requested that he was able to come and chat to us and thank us personally for the work we had done. I was the representative from the dog section. I had made sure that Jet had been fully groomed and his coat was lovely and glossy. As the Mayor approached, Jet decided he could wait no longer and squatted down to drop a lovely pile of poo on the pavement. Which from where I was standing seemed to smell more pungent than normal. This was just as the Mayor was about to speak to me. Trying to ignore Jet and the pile of poo. I just made polite conversation until he had passed. Sadly, not expecting Jet to leave a present on the pavement, I had not brought any 'dog bags' to pick his waste up in. I had to request someone go and get me a plastic bag from a local shop so I could clean up the mess. With VIPs and press present, I could not leave the mess, otherwise I am sure it would have been the next day's news headlines, "Police Office Does Not Get a Ticket for Leaving Dog Mess," or "Dog Cop Plop" along with pictures of myself and Jet. Thankfully, nothing further was said about the incident from anyone. They must have taken pity on poor Jet and his need to go to the loo...

***

We had been called to a male who had just robbed a post office, he had threatened staff with a baseball bat before running off. CCTV had picked him going into another building. A quite young in service inspector, thought he had jumped out of a window and made off. I knew full well that any person who jumped out of this building would fall straight into the canal, and being winter time would not survive for long in the cold water. I stated this to the Inspector, who was less than impressed and I continued to search the building with Jet. After ten minutes Jet barked and I went over to him. He was in a room with a desk and under hat desk. I found the Robber doing his very best to hide. I sent Jet in and he returned with the Robber. I immediately recognised him. His usual MO was to try and hide what he had just stolen, then after he had been released, would go back later and pick his 'booty' back up. "Warren, if you don't bring what you have nicked out with you, "I will set the dog on you," I said giving Jet the signal to be ready to go in. He did as he was told. I made Warren stand with his hands against the wall whilst I undertook a search and emptied all of Warren's pockets. All the time Jet kept watch, just in case Warren made a bid for freedom as he had done successfully on several occasions. Although with Jet standing guard close by, I doubt even Warren would have taken his chances. I handcuffed Warren to the rear and took a grip on the black plastic handle that sits in between the standard UK issue Quickcuff. Leading him out I took him straight to the Inspector, winked and said, "Sir, do you want this collar to go in your name or mine?" The Inspector looked a little sheepish and said, "Constable I will leave it to you to book him in my team will then come and interview him later. After we have got all the witness statements." "OK, Sir," I replied.

I placed him in the back of a local officer's police car and briefed them on his ability to escape before following the two local officers down to the custody, just in case Warren did try to escape. We made it to the custody suite and got Warren booked in for his overnight accommodation and free microwaved breakfast in the morning.

Not long after heading back out on the open road, I came across a car with its orange hazards, flashing away madly. The driver was, initially, nowhere to be seen. I was slightly concerned as the car was half on, half off a busy 60mph section of single carriage A road. As I was inspecting the car the driver turned up with a petrol can full of fuel. He said he had run out of fuel. I then noticed that he had not got the black funnel that you normally have with a petrol can. A colleague had once cut an old plastic Coke bottle, the kind you find in vending machines in half and then used that as a funnel. I scoured the side of the road to see if one had been discarded, and luckily I found a Fanta bottle of the same type as a Coke bottle. I promptly cut it in half with my trusty combi tool and gave it to the stranded motorist to use, in order to fill his car up, it worked a treat. It was not long before the car was back on its way and normal traffic flow could resume.

Back on the road it was not long until I got my next call to job of a missing child, missing children are another job that fills me with worry, especially a four year old boy, who had managed to unlock the front door, open it and wander out onto the street. I can imagine his mother being worried sick. We would like to find him as soon as possible, before any potential harm comes to him. Local officers were already searching the area and another officer was with the boy's mum trying to find out places he may try to go. Instinct told me to head for the local park and see if Jet could pick up a track, however, it would probably be best to start at the boy's house. I quickly got Jet out as time was of the essence, the more time that elapsed the further the boy could potentially travel. Jet seemed to pick up a scent straight away and he was off, I just hopped Jet had picked up the scent of the boy and not the postman or someone else how had visited the house.

We went down a couple of streets and even across a road before ending up at the park. At the park made straight for the play area. The play area was quite large with an area for toddlers with slides and sings and an area for older children, with a zip slide, swings climbing frame and slides. As I walked in I saw sitting on a swing amongst mothers and fathers with their children, a little boy matching description we had been given and Jet was tracking towards him. The boy was sitting merrily swinging backwards d forwards unaware of the commotion he had caused. I was amazed that none other parents had noticed a little boy on his own in the play area. Maybe they thought his parent or parents were sitting on one of the many seats around the play area. I passed the good news over the radio and could tell it was a big relief to all those involved. The boy took an instant liking to Jet and Jet seemed to understand this was a little boy who needed looking after. Jet kept a watchful eye on him as I walked the boy back home and into the arms of his joyful mother. The mother scooped the boy up in her arms for an enormous hug with tears flooding down her face before telling the boy off. A happy ending for all and Jet was the hero that quickly found the little boy safe and well.

Missing Person

The RSPCA does an excellent job. As an animal lover, I never like to see any animal suffer and further more hate to hear of any animal having to be put down. I know at times through suffering or the state of the animal there is little choice. I have been to several cases of animal neglect over the years, one were several dogs and been left in a shed, to basically die. I went along with the RSPCA after a tip off to find the decomposed bodies of three dogs. One riddled with maggots and another dog who was barely alive and tragically had to be put down. There is no excuse to leave a living creature in this state and show such a callous attitude towards them. Even after the discovery the couple felt they had done nothing wrong and did not know what all the fuss was about. At court they got a hefty fine and were banned from keeping animals for life. Even the police sometimes get it wrong after reading this story yesterday about a police force being forced to have their own sniffer dog put down after he was found to be an illegal breed.

"Officers at Avon and Somerset Police took on Tyson, a pitbull-cross, after he had appeared on a TV show. But despite showing "great potential" he had to be put to sleep at a Taunton RSPCA centre after officers found he was a banned breed.

A police dog specialist ruled Tyson, though a cross-breed, was still of the banned 'pitbull type' and he had to be returned to the West Hatch RSPCA centre near Taunton. Unable to legally rehome him under the Government's breed standard laws, the centre had no choice but to put him to sleep." Source: The Telegraph

I have often had the thought that after I retire I would love to do something with animals. It is a bit too late to become a vet even if I did have the brain power and A level grades. I would love to set up a training school for dogs and maybe kennels for them to stay when their owners were away on holiday. My wife thinks I am quite mad, but with the job I do, there are times I would much rather live with animals than humans.

I was on my second day shift of two. Response last night had been called out to reports of a missing elderly lady. She had been missing for five hours by about 8pm last night. The team had undertaken a thorough search and had both the police helicopter and dogs out searching for her. With the concern for her safety and rated as a risk missing person, all of the local Neighbourhood Police Teams had been tasked with conducting a large area search. I was told I would need to go for a briefing. With a rather large sigh, as he knew it would mean a day without being able to catch up with urgent paperwork, I got Jet sorted and jumped into the police car.

I made the seven-mile drive and got there just in time for the briefing. It was nice to see the rest of the NPT team, many of whom I had not seen for months. I have worked on operations with a number of them on quite a few occasions. The NPT Inspector was leading the briefing and had a picture of a really sweet old lady on the interactive whiteboard. She was suffering from dementia, which added to the concerns about her being out in what had been a wet and cold night.

Many thought that she may already be dead, but did not want to say it out loud. The tone of the room was quite sombre as everyone took down all the information. Including when she was last seen and where she might have gone. A satellite view of the area was put on the interactive whiteboard and it was clear to see that this would not be an easy search, simply judging by the type of ground we would need to search. The chances of Jet being able to pick up a decent scent, seemed remote due to the amount of rain we had had overnight. Normally, I would have started where she was last seen, but decided our best bet was to cover an area that had not already been searched ad take it from there.

The retirement home, she had gone missing from was almost in the middle of nowhere. It was surrounded by fields and the odd few large clumps of trees dotted around on quite a rolling area of land. The woman's details had already been splashed across local TV screens and mentioned on the radio to allow members of the public to be aware and keep an eye out for her.

We had a couple of police vans to take us out to our various assigned search areas. Although I would use my car to transport Jet. I could see this being a very long and tiresome day in poor conditions. Searches of this type could be hard going; they were physically demanding, especially on more difficult terrain, and could be emotionally draining too, especially if it was for a vulnerable person, as you knew that each hour that passed the chances of finding them alive diminished.

As we all travelled towards the search area control suddenly came over the radio to say that a dog walker had found an old lady covered in mud and lying in a puddle at the edge of a field. About half a mile away from the retirement home. Everyone assumed she was dead. An ambulance was travelling and the police van's blue lights and whaler were activated to get to the scene quicker. I took the lead having the faster vehicle and sped off towards the dog walker.

On arrival, I could see an ambulance crew in the distance. They were easy to make out due their distinctive green uniforms. I got out and left Jet in the car, no point getting him covered in mud just yet. The field was very muddy and after just a few feet, my boots, along with the bottom of my trousers, were covered in mud. It was quite a walk to get over to the elderly woman, and it must have been quite a walk for her. The ground was very sodden and it took quite a bit of effort to pull each foot back out of the mud.

As I got over, I realised much to my relief that the woman was still alive, suffering from exposure and looking rather dishevelled with her nightie caked in mud. She was only just conscious and was still not out of the woods yet. Due to the distance from the road and the difficulty in getting her to the ambulance the air ambulance was called in. It would have to land and hover at the same time to ensure it did not sink into the mud.

Within ten minutes, this bright yellow helicopter was overhead battering us with the down blast from its rotors as it tried to find the best place to land. With the ground being so sodden it could not fully land and would have to hover just touching the field. As the helicopter would have most certainly sunk into the soft sticky mud. Wrapped in a space blanket, the elderly lady, still shivering, had become slightly more conscious, which was a good sign. She was placed on a stretcher and I carried her with the air ambulance crew the very short distance through the mud to the helicopter, before being whisked away to the local hospital. I later heard that she made a full recovery, although she was unable to remember anything. A good result all round and we were more than thankful to the member of public finding her. I doubt the elderly lady would have survived much longer in the elements.

ACC

The ACC (Assistant Chief Constable) was due to visit the kennels in the morning for an inspection and see how Force funds were being spent on the dog section. We were told to make sure all our dogs were well-groomed, announced by the section Sgt. Our Sgt was a cop of twenty five years and had excellent knowledge of the law. He was a great skipper and had been a dog handler for 10 years. He was not one for bending over backwards for senior officers. To him supporting us in order to support the police officers out on the front line was his prime concern. In theory the purpose of the inspection was to see that the kennels were clean and the dogs well-groomed and looking healthy. Why then was I the only handler other than the ACC to be present at the inspection? The answer was that as many as possible made sure they were on an operation, training or anything but being present at the kennels, even the Sgt had turned sideways and disappeared. To be honest, I liked the ACC he was a very pleasant and understanding senior officer, he was impressed by how clean the kennels were and even more impressed with the fact that everyone was out doing something on his visit! I decided to just say that we were a popular and very busy resource. We went to the kennels and walked passed each kennel most of them empty, but a few with dogs in, who all started to bark at the sight of the ACC. Maybe the dogs knew or sensed something about him that I did not know?

The ACC stopped at one Kennel and asked "Is this the new dog?" "No, Sir that belongs to Inspector Riley we are looking after it whilst he is on holiday," I replied. "Oh, I did not realise we ran a dog holiday home, how much are we charging." "Err nothing, Sir" I replied. "Oh, I think I shall be having words on his return, money is tight as it is, without the force giving free board and lodgings to any old mutt." I decided to say nothing more, as was not prepared to implicate myself any further. I decided to direct the ACC to one of our new cars that we had only received last week. With that the ACC hurried off to his next meeting impressed with the dog section, although I would not like to see the email that Inspector Riley would find in his inbox on his return from holiday.

With the inspection over, it was amazing to see how many handlers suddenly reappeared! Although they at least brought me some breakfast and a coffee, as payment for services rendered. It was not long before it was back to the grindstone and I was racing out to another job. This was for a runner from a car that had contained a couple of joyriders. The passenger had been caught quite easily, as she had decided to stay in the car knowing full well we could not prove she had actually done anything wrong. The driver of the car had made off into a slightly less affluent estate with a couple of police officers chasing after him. The police officers had lost him in the back alleys of the estate. It would be Jet's job to pick up the track and hopefully find the joyrider so I could arrest him. I radioed on ahead to ask the officers to stop searching for him, so not confuse the dog by laying down multiple tracks. My best guess was that he had gone to ground either in a property or hidden in a garden, not far from where the police officers last saw him.

I quickly got Jet out the back of the car and attached his long lead. Before taking him up the alley where the driver of the stolen car, had last been seen. Jet seemed to pick up a track straight away and headed off down another alleyway, before turning around and going part way back the way he came. He then started to bark at a back gate, a sign that there may be something behind it. I opened the wooden gate and it creaked loudly as it opened, if the driver had not heard Jet barking he would have heard the bloomin gate opening. Jet was straight into the garden and after a quick scout around started to scratch at a grey wheelie bin, in the corner of the garden, near to the rear of the house. I quickly opened the lid to the wheelie bin and sure enough crouched down inside was a slightly frightened teenage boy, who on getting out I noticed was covered in household waste including last night's takeaway in the form of a curry. So he smelt awful and looked in quite a sorry state as I helped him climb out. Even Jet found him a bit whiffy and seemed to want to stand away from the teenager as best as he could, still barking excitedly.

A local officer heard me shout and soon hot footed it to me in the garden. He swiftly handcuffed the lad before taking him to the police car and onto the custody suite. With all the local police now tied up with the joyriders, the minute I went "State 2." I got asked if I could help out with an RTC that had just come in, on a quite rolling country road, about 2 miles away from my location. This road was notorious for accidents, several of which had proved fatal. So when it came in a car had left the road I did fear the worst. It was hard to find the accident initially, but two young people appeared at the roadside and I thought these must have witnessed the crash. The two lads in their early twenties had actually been involved in the crash. I could just see the car on its side half way down the field or bout 300m from where it had gone through the hedge and barrel rolled down the hill. It was amazing that both the occupants had escaped uninjured. Due to the manner of the crash, I wanted Ambulance to come out and check them over. Whilst waiting I asked the driver what had happened, he said "dunno, I just came over the brow of the hill and the car veered off the road." "What speed were you going?" I asked. "Only about 30 to 40 mph."

"There is no way you were doing 30-40 mph looking at where the car had ended up, I would have suggested at least 60mph which is the speed limit for the road." The driver did not reply, just had a very sheepish look on his face.

Ambulance then turned up and started to check the occupants over for any pains or potential non visible injuries, the ambulance crew looked at the car and said how lucky they had been, injury wise. As I was talking, I noticed a tyre mark on the other side of the road that went into the grass verge. At the top of the hill there was another mark on the side of the road, on the side they would have been driving. It seemed like they had come up the hill a little too fast, most likely taken some air and come back down clipping the grass verge. Which had then sent the car to the other side of the road, the driver would have corrected, possibly over corrected and the car bounced back across the road and through the hedge before barrel rolling several times down the hill.

I walked up to the very sorry looking car, as I walked towards it, I passed one of the front wheels complete with suspension and drive shaft still attached, then walked past the front and rear bumper. The car looked brand new and a quick check on the vehicle registration number or VRM, revealed it to be a Vauxhall Corsa SXi, now almost certainly a write off. It had protected its occupants well, though. The driver told me he had only had it two days. His parent hen turned up looking less than impressed, but glad he was OK. His insurance would take a hammering and his dad said he will have to do without a car for a while. There was no evidence or witnesses to be able to prosecute for any road traffic offence, or even suggest that one had been committed. To be fair with the loss of his car and hike in his insurance premium, the driver was already going to suffer. Thankfully, without suffering any injuries, although I think he may well feel a little stiff the next morning.

New Arrival

Jet and I have been put in to help cover a local football match. There was intelligence to say that rival fans planned to take on the local fans. This meant extra public order officers had been drafted in. Jet even with vast angry crowds still stays calm and fully controllable. Even if he does bark if anyone gets a little too close for comfort. The noise can be a little intense at times, though, with all the shouting and roars from the crowd. A dog's hearing is up to fifty times more sensitive than ours. Jet does one of his stretches in front of the crowd almost to show how calm and relaxed he is. Starting with his bottom up high and head down, before stretching his front legs out before sitting back down on his bottom and head held up high. The match goes off without a hitch and the away fans are kept in a strict cordon and escorted in the opposite direction to the home fans.

Other than the odd slight scuffle that Jet soon sorted with the odd snarl or two, or the away fans are boarded onto buses and trains. As soon as we were stood down I took Jet for a walk and a play with his ball in the local park for both of us to relax and wind down. I got home that night, to the best news ever, Mrs Blackshaw was pregnant and I was soon to become a father. A mixture of emotions cascaded through me, elation at having a child, worry as to how Jet would get on with the child, the financial aspect and finally the euphoria a man feels when his seeds have produced offspring. I suppose a good dose of male ego.

Over the next few months Jet did sense a change in the house and he knew that something was going to happen. The spare room, went from guest room to nursery and once he knew we were having a boy, the clothes and toys which my wife insisted on buying just in case he baby came 'tomorrow' even though she had two months to go. Work, in some respects took a back seat, my focus was on preparing to be a dad and at the same time giving Jet plenty of TLC, as I did not want him to feel left out in any way.

I was at work when I got the call to say my wife needed me urgently. Thankfully, I was not at a job and I was able to go state 11, police speak for going off duty. The baby was three days late. The baby seemed in no hurry to meet its parents. Up until now, my wife's pregnancy had been straightforward, but when she went to the clinic today the doctor was a little concerned about the size of the baby.

She was booked in for an ultrasound at the hospital. The news was that the baby's head was very low and that it roughly weighed a manageable 7lbs 8oz - so far so good. She checked in at the maternity ward of the hospital, where the midwife did a quick internal examination.

"Actually, you're three centimetres dilated already," the midwife said with a smile.

That was the first in a series of shocks that we were to experience over the next four days.

I was desperately looking forward to meeting my son, I had found it hard to grasp the concept that the lump in my wife's stomach was actually going to become this baby. Through all the sickness, backache, swollen ankles and relentless kicking, Mrs Blackshaw had already formed a very close bond with her "bump."

"Go home and if nothing happens overnight, come in tomorrow morning at nine," said the midwife. So back home, we went. There was no point going on duty and decided to start my two weeks paternity leave there and then. Everything seemed to be going fine at home, and despite the fact my wife was three centimetres dilated, she wasn't in any pain, so she wondered quite seriously whether she was going to be one of the lucky few who experienced a 'silent labour'.

A couple of hours later she had some bleeding, and, staying close to the instructions in all the books and what the midwife ad advised, I rang the hospital to say we were on our way. They wanted to keep her in overnight. I was sent home and spent a restless night at home without my wife for the first time since we had been married, waiting for a phone call to say she had gone into labour. However, it never came, which meant I made my way back to the hospital the next morning. Where I was fully expecting her to be induced.

For some unknown reason, countless other couples seemed to have the same due date as us, and it was like a national birth weekend at the hospital. We had to wait early on Sunday morning for a space on the maternity ward. I found it a nerve-wracking few days and was thoroughly exhausted with worry. In between, I had to pop back home and take Jet to the HQ kennels, as Jet would be better cared for there, but I felt so guilty in leaving him. I really felt he should be there at the birth a part of the family, but that was completely against all hospital regulations.

Nearly three days later than expected, my wife's waters finally broke while she was waiting to be induced. I had never seen anything like it; I could not believe she had managed to keep what appeared to be two or three large bucketful's of liquid inside her for so long.

As time went on, she started having mild contractions, combined with a return of the back pain she'd had earlier in the pregnancy. Gradually, the contractions intensified and, with the back pain causing her to be sick, she decided she needed an epidural. I had felt like a spare part during most of her nine-month pregnancy, but right now I felt truly useless and the feeling got worse. There was not much I could do but hold her hand and keep talking to her about totally random stuff.

She found it easier to push whilst on her side, and she was doing really well. I remember speaking to a colleague on my old shift who had been quite embarrassed at managing to pass out during his daughter's birth. This same colleague had been called to sudden deaths, stabbings and fatal RTCs, only to succumb to the birth of his own daughter. Thinking of this had made me feel a bit nervous about watching the delivery. However, once the midwife said she could see the top of the head, I could not resist having a peek. My wife wanted to know exactly what I had seen, was there any hair, if so what colour, was his head OK.

Despite my feelings of inadequacy, the midwife encouraged me to be as involved as possible. Not only did I try to offer words of support from time to time, even whilst my wife was swearing like a trooper, I was given the task of preparing the newborn baby's clothes and putting bedding in the cot. I was also asked if I wanted to cut the cord once the baby had been delivered.

She needed an episiotomy to make things easier, and after less than an hour's pushing, at 1.58am, baby Benjamin shot out into the delivery room - a whopping 8lbs 15oz. To my immense relief, baby Ben started to cry almost immediately. I had just watched my son emerge into the world; it was a fantastic, frightening, exhilarating experience which I felt privileged to have witnessed. Both myself and my wife felt elated and tears came to both of our eyes, even though I fought hard to hold my tears back. The feeling of euphoria hit me once again and felt so elated and so proud to be a father.

Once Ben had been born, my automatic reaction was to relax, but it was not over yet. As the placenta was delivered, my wife lost quite a lot of blood. Her blood pressure plummeted and before I knew it, I was in the middle of a scene from Casualty, and literally left holding the baby while four or five staff gave the necessary aid to her.

She needed four units of blood and was not allowed back onto the ward until she had had an operation for a retained placenta, as not all of the placenta had come out during childbirth. With my wife was being told to rest, I was given basic lessons in bathing, dressing, and nappy changing; the upside was at least I had the opportunity to get to know my baby son and be of some practical use.

A day or so later, after my wife had recovered enough to be allowed home. I was finally able to realise that I had become a father. I started to enjoy being woken up every two or three hours for Benjamin to feed. It was much easier to be at work than at home with a new born baby though. I took my share of feeds when my wife switched from breast milk to formula. As for Jet, he took to Ben straight away and was very protective, especially outside, if anyone approached the pram to have a look at Ben he would growl and snarl. I would have to tell him off, even though I know he was just protecting his family. Having a child really does turn your life upside and those first few months with sleep deprivation and the constant demands of a baby can make tempers fray. This is where Jet was a good mediator, always reminding us of what we should and should not be focusing on. I think overall Jet dealt better with the new arrival than we did!

Jet to the Rescue

Around all the joys of a new baby there was something more sinister around the corner. Just after Ben's first birthday, I noticed that Jet seemed to be going to the toilet more often. Initially, I thought it was Jet getting older, so I ignored it, but it seemed to be getting worse. On his next check up with the vet, I asked him to take a look, he just thought it was a bladder infection so prescribed Jet antibiotics. The problem, then seemed to get better so again we carried on for a few more months when it returned only this time much worse. Jet was constantly trying to wee, to the point he would sometimes only go ten feet before trying to wee again. I took him back to the vets who checked him out and prescribed another course of antibiotics. This time they had no effect and within two weeks we were back at the vets for X-rays. What was found shocked the vet more than me. Jet had got quite a large stone in his bladder which in turn was reducing his bladder capacity. It was the actual size that shocked the vet the most. The stone was the size of a small stone some 2 cm in width and 4 cm in length. It meant Jet would need surgery as soon as possible. I was worried sick about Jet and the fact he had to have an operation. He could go under the knife the next day and I had to leave him at the vets overnight. I felt sorry for Jet and for having to leave him at the vets, but knew it would be for the best. Jet was in the best of hands, but it did not stop me from having a sleepless night as a worried father.

The next day Jet went under anaesthetic to have an operation to remove the stone. I got a call later on at work to say Jet was fine and now recovering from his operation. The relief was immense and I was pleased that Jet would be OK, he was my best friend, my partner and, to be quite honest I do not know how I would manage without him. To loose Jet would be like losing a loved one. My wife was also quite worried, although she did her best to hide it. Jet would not be operational for at least three weeks and would then need to be assessed that he was fit for duty. He would also have to pass a series of tests to check his performance, control and tracking abilities. I knew he would be fine, but again the worrier inside me had thoughts, "what will I do if he does not pass?" "Could I manage to take on and train another dog?" I knew that one day I would,

As Jet would retire and then I would need a new partner. Although Jet's retirement could only ever be with him living with us seeing out his final years. I must admit if I had not got into the dog unit I may well be doing something different. As much as I love police work, the high stress levels and greatly reduced manpower, stretching each individual police officer further. I may well have decided to change careers as a few have of those that started with me. One resigned to join the Airport Fire Brigade and loves the slightly slower pace of life and not being verbally and physically abused. Jet takes on some of my workload and pressure at the same time being a great stress reducer and helping to keep me calm. I let him do all the loud barking and growling whilst I stay totally calm and never raise my voice.

Three weeks later, Jet was passed as fit for duty and quite excited to be getting back out onto the front line. He was far too active to not be working and I could tell Jet seemed a little depressed. Back on nights, it was just after 4am just as things were starting to slow down, when I got a call to a pub that was being burgled. The pub, called the Sun Inn, was on the far side of the county, but only a 5 minute's drive from my location. On this shift, I seemed to have spent more time on blue lights than not. So far, I had used over three quarters of a tank of fuel. On arrival at the Sun Inn, I jumped out and climbed over a fence whilst another officer who had just turned up went round the front.

I climbed through the smashed window and made his way into the pub. As soon as I got in, I found the landlord at the bottom of the stairs in the hall. He told me that the offenders had already left. Anxious to get after them, I took some basic details. The landlord told me that he had held the door to his flat above the pub shut whilst burglars tried to smash the door in. After a while, the burglars had given up and fled empty-handed. The landlord then showed me the crowbar and torch they had left behind.

"Scenes of crime may be able to get some evidence off them, just don't touch it, I get an officer to come and seize them" I said.

With basic details collected and local police officers on scene to get a witness statement, I went on an area search. As I drove off a report of a second pub burglary quickly came in. This was only just down the road from the Sun Inn and too much of a coincidence not to be the same offenders. Once again, we sped off and within a couple of minutes we were at the Dog and Duck. On arrival, I saw that a window had been smashed and got Jet out to as backup and to see if we could catch anyone. Just as we were about to enter Jet barked and drew my attention to the pub car park at the rear.

In the car park, a silver MKII Audi A3 on false number plates was revving its engine and spinning its wheels throwing up dark grey smoke, before heading towards me and Jet to get away. As the car screeched past me, I managed to smash the passenger window with my baton before they escaped.

The registration number came back as a different colour Audi A3, which had its number plates stolen earlier that day from a house on the other side of the city.

We ran back to our car and radioed in all the details on the burglars whilst we tried to re-locate the car. We tried the main roads first, but there was no sign of them. We then doubled back round the housing estate and locally-known hiding places, but again to no avail. It was looking like a total loss, when reports came in that local officers had found an abandoned Audi A3. It was most likely to be the same car that had made off from me. Jet an I raced to where the car had been found, and it was time to put Jet to the test for the first time this shift. For some reason I really wanted to catch these two burglars, maybe because they had tried to run Jet down. Jet seemed to pick up a track straight away that went down to where the road ended and into a freshly ploughed field, that was baked hard due to the recent lack of rain.

We quickly made our way across the field and ended up in a wood that was very dark due to the thick tree canopy. Jet headed into the wood and when we were about 100 m into the wood I heard a "WHACK" and felt a hard blow to the back of my head, I felt dazed and dropped to the floor just making out Jet barking, before passing out. When I came to, my vision was slightly blurred and could make out the outline of Jet and two men he was fighting with. As my vision came back, I could see one of the men swinging a crowbar at Jet, the same crowbar that had most likely been used to whack me on my head, fearing for Jet's safety, I hit the orange emergency button on my Sepura radio. Instantly, the radio went quiet and gave me ten seconds of air priority. In a groggy voice I said "I......neeeed assistance, woods at my location, beeeeen attacked." The dispatcher acknowledged my call, and got units to travel, thankfully a local unit had found my police car after I radioed in the location of the abandoned car and had started to make their way across the field as my assistance call came in. When you hear an officer in need of assistance, everyone in the area stops what they are doing and makes their way to help. You know seconds count and it is a fellow officer who needs help, usually with no one else able to help.

As I was a dog unit under attack, all sorts of resources started to make their way, knowing it must be serious if a dog and its handler was in need of assistance. By now my vision was much better, but still not good enough to be able to use my Taser. Jet was courageously still fighting with the two men, enduring kicks and punches long with the odd whack from the crowbar. The two men had no idea I was conscious as I tried to get up and protect Jet. Finally, I could hear two other officers puffing and panting as they ran towards me. It seemed like I had been there ages when in reality it had only been a few minutes. They rushed in and pulled one of the men off with Jet still attached, Jet released him and then went and dug his teeth into the other male as he tried to escape. I knew I had to go in and help Jet. I staggered towards Jet and the male, with Jet tenaciously hanging onto the male's leg. All I could do as draw my ASP and with a very poor aim, whack him as hard as I could. I had aimed for the shoulder, but my poor aim meant I hit his head and knocked him out cold. He fell to the floor with a thud and a rustle of leaves. The other male was fighting hard with the other two officers, but was fighting a losing battle pinned to the floor, they soon had him handcuffed, just as a couple of armed response officers arrived.

They first came over to check on me, "Are you alright mate?" "I think so, I took a whack to the head, is Jet OK?" I said.

"I can see some blood on the back of your head mate, you need to sit down and I will get an ambulance." I just said quite angrily, "Forget about me, WHAT ABOUT JET?"

I think they could tell I was suffering from concussion and just said "Jet is fine, looks like he has put up one hell of a fight.

After that, I must have passed out again, as I woke up in hospital with a thumping headache. I was made to stay in all of the next day before being released. It was not until my Sgt had come to visit me, was I told of Jet's heroic actions. He had suffered cuts, bruises and a broken rib as he tried to both protect and apprehend the burglars. The burglars had suffered multiple dog bites on their legs, hands and feet. Jet had not only protected me, but also apprehended two burglars on his own. The two offenders were not only charged with burglary, but also resisting arrest, assaulting a police officer and police dog which amounted to GBH (Grevious Bodily Harm) under Section 18 which reads as "Whosoever shall unlawfully and maliciously by any means whatsoever wound or cause any grievous bodily harm to any person, . . . with intent, . . . to do some . . . grievous bodily harm to any person, or with intent to resist or prevent the lawful apprehension or detainer of any person, shall be guilty of felony, and being convicted thereof shall be liable . . . to be kept in penal servitude for life . . ."

They are currently away at her majesties pleasure after their day in Crown Court, and both got nine years. Myself and Jet both got a commendation from the Chief Constable for apprehending the two burglars, although Jet was the real hero and did much more and suffered more than me, and for that I don't think he will ever know how proud and thankful I am of him.

Sadly, Jet passed away at the end of December 2014 aged 11, after suffering from gastric torsion. He retired just past his eighth birthday after a very successful career as a police dog. This book is dedicated to man's best friend, both a companion and work partner. Jet will forever be loved and never be forgotten. He always will be my hero and an irreplaceable dog. Rest in peace in doggy heaven, we will meet again someday…

Short UK Police Dog History

The British Police dog can trace its roots back to a vague entry in 1859, when police officers in Luton acquired a blood hound and used it to aid in trying to solve a murder. Dogs have for many centuries worked alongside humans as loyal and hardworking partners. They are naturally good at tracking, guarding and communicating along with companionship. The earliest recorded usage of dogs is by the Greeks who used them in battle - the Romans also used dogs in battle who wore armour.

The earliest reports of police dog use outside of Britain, goes back to the 15th Century. It is thought that dogs accompanied Parish Constables when they went out on patrol, especially in the evening. Although, the belief is that these dogs were used more as company for the Parish Constable than working dogs.

British police dogs initially had very little training and again were more for companionship than for police work. Many constables took their own dogs out on patrol with them. Dog's however, we're still seen as an encumbrance as opposed to an asset and some forces such as Northumberland in the 1870s were told to suspend any police officer found on duty with their dog. This restriction stayed in place until 1910. The first real use of a British police dog was in the 1880s where Sir Charles Warran used a Blood Hound to try and help solve the Jack the Ripper murders in London. However, the commissioner was bitten by one of the dogs, who then, promptly ran off together, requiring a police search to find them, giving the dogs some negative press. In the 1890s, Hyde Park police station had a Fox Terrier called Topper, who often joined officers on their evening patrols. Due to Topper being untrained, he was of little use and in some police circles seen as more of a publicity stunt than anything else.

The use of dogs abroad was much more rapid abroad than in Britain. In the 1890s in Germany, training programs for dogs were introduced. In 1897, Franz Laufer Prussian Police Inspector had the idea of using dogs to escort police officers to ward off attackers. This idea came to him after several attacks on police officers on the night shift. Initial scepticism was rife; however, Franz pursued his idea, even with very little knowledge of dogs and was given a grant in 1900 to purchase three dogs. He would need assistance as there were no books or experts around. So Franz recruited a Sgt who had worked with dogs when he was a gamekeeper before becoming a police officer. He knew straight away that a German Shepard would be the best type of dog to have as a police dog. Franz thought that the Great Dane would be more intimidating to would be attackers though.

Franz believed that dogs could be used not just for protecting people, but also tracking individuals. In 1901, Franz's first police dog, a Great Dane called Ceaser joined the police. The dog was muzzled and kept on a lead at all times. The public was dubious until Ceaser had proved is worth by tracking a criminal over two miles. In 1899 the German Shepherd Dog Society was formed and in 1903 they had a series of trials showing off how German Shepherds with various exercises following scents and showing how well a German Shepherd could be controlled. The police were impressed, but they were not convinced the cost of training the dogs was worth it.

In a town in Belgium called Ghent, the police chief was leading the way of the employment of police dogs from around 1859. He used them also to accompany police officers on night patrol. He used Belgium Sheepdogs due to their ability to be well trained and become highly effective. The police chief Van-Wessmael believed that the dogs possessed a number of qualities that made them effective in the fight against crime. They were cheaper to deploy than more officers on patrol. The dogs could pursue an offender more quickly than a police officer using their good hearing and great ability to pick up a scent. Finally, they had the agility to follow offenders over obstacles. Such was Van-Wessmaels faith in dogs, that the force soon had 69 of them.

Police dogs in the UK were still of little interest to police forces, who could not see the point or need in them. It took a dog trainer from the Army, a Colonel Richardson to persuade the police the benefits of having police dogs. Pointing out the work carried out by police dogs in Germany and Belgium. It was suggested that the Metropolitan Police had its own dog section, but after a visit to France in 1906, representatives from the force came back unimpressed. Also in 1906, a Chief Goods Manager for Hull docks in Yorkshire, visited Ghent - by chance, he was able to see the police dogs in action and was so impressed. On his return to Hull he spoke to the Superintendent who was responsible for policing the docks in Hull. The Chief Goods Manager was able to convince the Superintendant that dogs would be a real asset in helping his police officers protect the docks. The Superintendant also visited Ghent along with some other police officers and was impressed enough to set up his own dog section. In 1908 police dogs started patrolling the docks in Hull, initially with four dogs. The scheme was then extended to Hartlepool Docks and a short time later Tyne and Middlesborough Docks. The dogs were only used at night and not always by the same police officer. The dogs were trained to recognise a police uniform and attack anyone who was not wearing a uniform.

In 1910, Major Richardson wrote to every constabulary in the UK, informing them of the success of police dogs abroad. As a respected military dog trainer, some Chief Constables started to take steps to set up small dog units with their force. In 1913 the Chief Constable of West Riding, Yorkshire expressed his support for any police officers wishing to train dogs to assist them and the role of the police dog began to develop. A year later, Major Richardson addressed the members of the Chief Constable Association during which he highlighted the benefits of using police dogs. He also classified e dogs into either night patrol dogs, or dogs used to track criminals down. Ghent had become a showcase for what police dogs could do. By World War I, dogs were being trained for military use as guards and sentries. The German Shepherd was used extensively by the Germans on the Western Front. The British and USA, picked up on their use in the military and 10 dogs from the Hull docks were quickly conscripted into the Army. The success of the 'dock dogs' meant more and more docks started to use dogs for night patrols. The training of the 'dock dogs' continued to be developed during the war years and by the end of World War I, 185 suspects had been captured by the 'dock dogs.'

This still, did not create a bigger uptake of police dogs by other police forces. To become a police dog, a dog would have to complete 83 exercises to a high standard. During the 1920s, various breeds, including the Great Dane, Doberman, Retriever, Bull Mastiff and Mastiff were used. In 1923 the dog section was put under review and the decision made to use German Shepherds by the trainers. It was a breed that was still quite rare at that time in Britain, and the Bull Mastiff was also popular as a tracking dog. It was not until the late 1920s that the general police constabularies became interested in police dogs and it took until 1934 for a committee to be set up to evaluate the use and training of police dogs. The concern was that dogs could harm the public/police relationship. But a report on Europe persuaded them to carry out experiments in the breeding and training of police dogs. The following year the Metropolitan Police Force took on two Labradors, who commenced patrols on the streets of Brixham and Southhawk in 1938. At the outbreak of war with the experiment at an end the two dogs were handed to the Cheshire Constabulary. During the Second World War, the number of dogs being used by the police dropped significantly. The main reason was that many dogs were registered for national service. After being used in the First World War the decision was made to use only certain dog breeds, with duties ranging from mine detection to guarding buildings. The training for the dogs was intense, those that did not make the grade were returned home. After the end of the Second World War, interest in using police dogs was renewed. Partly due to rising crime rates, especially in London. In 1946 the Metropolitan Police acquired four Labrador puppies for training. It was decided that for the training to be successful, each dog would be appointed one dog handler and the dog would live with its handler. In 1947, he Chief Constable of Surrey became interested in having police dogs and appointed a PC from Scotland Yard, who favoured the use of German Shepherd dogs. He was instructed by the Chief Constable to set up a police dog section based on the continental approach to training and breeding. On 27th September 1950 Surrey opened its own dog training school in Guildford. Within the next four years the majority of larger police forces had established dog section. The use of police dogs grew at a rapid rate. In 1955 it was agreed by all the training schools that a standardised training program was required to fully develop a dog and make best use of their abilities for police work. The training program focused especially on searching, tracking and control.

In 1958, this training program was taken to the Home Office Committee on police dogs, whose purpose was to advise n police dogs at a national level. During the 1960s, significant developments in the training and deployment of police dogs. In 1963 a training manual for police dogs was introduced covering training and care and then in 1964 a national course for instructors was introduced. As the role of the police dog has grown, so has the use of specialist dogs to search for drugs, money, explosives, weapons and human remain detection. Today there is around 2500 police dogs amongst the 43 UK Police Forces, with the German Shepherd being the most popular breed used.

Appendix - Types of Police Dogs
German Shepherd

The German Shepherd is probably the most recognisable of all the police dogs. Their dark tan, brown and black colouring, with alert pointed ears, that gives the breed an almost Wolf like appearance. They are a very loyal and obedient breed and make very good working dogs due to their intelligence, agility and strength. They are very graceful and fast, always wanting to please and protect their owners. German Shepherds are eager to learn and respond well to training, learning quickly. They excel at tracking as well as chasing and detaining suspects. They form a close bond with their trainer or handler making for a very close working relationship.

Rottweiler

The Rottweiler tends to have a bit of a bad reputation, due to their nature. However, much of this is down to their owners and how they have treated them. They need to be handled and trained well due to their size, otherwise they can become powerful and aggressive. With short black hair and brown markings, with a broad head and forward carried ears and a docked tail, are easily recognisable. The Rottweiler is a devoted dog and has become misunderstood. They have a balanced temperament, but will protect and defend their owners, which is where some of the bad reputation has come from. They like companionship a are very loyal and quite easy to train. They must be trained when they are young, so the trainer becomes the pack leader. This helps the Rottweiler learn to obey. Once properly trained, a Rottweiler is good with other pets and children. They also make for excellent general purpose police dogs.

Giant Schnauzer

The Giant Schnauzer is not a dog normally associated as a police dog. They are a loyal and loving dog that rarely leave their owner's side. They stand square in stature, usually being as high as they are long.

They have a large head and a wiry coat that can be black or salt and pepper. They also have bushy eyebrows, whiskers and a beard with a large black nose. They need to be properly trained in much the same way as a Rottweiler. As the Giant Schnauzer is a very spirited and bold dog. They have to be very well socialised in order not to be suspicious of other people. Its large size is very good at deterring criminals, especially when they are being chased. They have a very loud bark and are very good as guard dogs. They were used during both of the World Wars, which reduced the numbers as to put the breed in jeopardy of extinction.

Doberman

The Doberman's full name is Doberman Pinscher. It is an elegant and powerful dog with a muscular body. It has short black, black and tan, white, and bluish grey. They are most commonly known for their appearances in a variety of films, normally the black or black and tan variety. They have most commonly been bred as guard dogs. But they are a very versatile dog. They are devoted and watchful and take good care of their owners. They are not a vicious dog either. They are highly intelligent and easy to train, with great energy, stamina and strength. Dobermans like human contact and do not like to be left alone. Their skills as well as guarding include tracking and search and rescue.

Labrador

The English Labrador is a heavy dog, which is larger and heavier than its American cousin. It can be coloured, black, chocolate or a sandy yellow colour. Its broad head sits on muscular neck with a thick nose and wide muzzle. Labradors have soft, intelligent eyes and a thick and strong tail. They are very adept at swimming due to the otter like tail and webbed feet. They are a very affectionate and patient dog. They are loyal and loving which means they like to play and are very good with children and pets. They will bark at new people before welcoming them, so do not make very good guard dogs. They are very easy to train though and need to be socialised as puppies to be more amenable to strangers. They are more usually seen as guide dogs or service dogs for disabled people. The Labrador is very good at hunting, tracking, retrieving, narcotics detection, bomb detection and search and rescue, it is an essential worker for the police.

Belgian Shepherd Dog

The Belgian Shepherd is another dog not normally associated with police work, but is used quite regularly. The Belgian Shepherd is black and muscular, agile and proportioned to appear very proud. It has erect triangular ears and a tapering muzzle. It has a mid-length coat with a neck ruff and feathering on its belly, tail and legs. There are four types of Belgian Shepherd, the Groenendael is the most popular. Belgian Shepherds are very territorial, serious and productive. They are also very obedient and intelligent. Like other breeds, it needs to be socialised as a puppy to stop it from becoming shy or over sensitive. They are good working dogs having plenty of energy and need to work to burn all that energy off. They tend to bond to only one or two people and can be overbearing to smaller dogs and pets. As they are good at herding they tend to circle and nip at the heels. This behaviour can be overcome with training. It is a good swimmer ad protective of its owner, and overall makes a good, general police dog.

Springer Spaniel

Springer Spaniels are employed for their sniffing abilities. They are trained to detect certain smells and then indicate when they find the smell. Being a small dog makes them ideal for sniffing out in tight places. They are about the smallest breed used by police. They have drop long down ears and a squarish body. They can be black and white, liver and white. They have a very loving look on their faces that usually melts an owner's heart. They can move quickly over the ground and are hard working dogs that are active and strong willed. They are a very loving and affectionate family dog. They have a steady temperament and are very social. They can become bored and that is usually when behavioural problems start. It needs early obedience and training to be successful as a police dog.

Appendix II – Basic Dog Commands

Sit

This is perhaps the most basic command given to a dog and is simply to get the dog to stop and sit, waiting for its next command. Many of the other commands build on this simple first command. It can also be given from the 'heel' command when the dog is walking. As the dog gets better at sitting the trainer will walk away, leaving the dog sitting. It is important that the dog learns to sit in a comfortable position, if the dog is not correctly seated, the trainer needs to correct the dog's position.

Heel

With this command a dog learns to walk on the lead, first on the left side of the trainer, with the dogs right shoulder close to the trainer's knee. The lead should be slack to leave enough room for the trainer to be able to pull on the lead to correct the dog. The lead should be held in the right hand, so that the left hand is free to praise the dog. The dog will soon learn the correct position will be more comfortable than pulling and will not please the trainer. Whilst on the lead once it has been mastered the dog can then learn to vary pace and direction according to what commands the dog is given. Once mastered with a lead the trainer can teach the dog to heel without a lead, however the lead should still be visible.

Stand

This command is given when he dog is on the 'heel' command with the lead. The trainer stops walking, gives the command 'stand' and holds their hand out in front of the dog's face. Once the dog has learned to stand, the trainer walks away and leaves the dog in this position. Then the trainer returns and gives the heel command for the dog to continue walking.

Down

The down command is aimed at having the dog lie down in a prone position instantly, whether the dog is at a distance or next to the trainer. The command is taught on the lead, but should also be practised with the dog off the lead. In order for the dog to understand what the 'down' command means, the trainer should give the command at the same time as applying gentle downward pressure on the dog's upper back and pulling downwards on a shortened lead. As soon as the dog is correctly lying down, the trainer must release the pressure. Once the dog responds to the command, all physical pressure can discontinue.

Distance Control

Once a dog has successfully learned basic commands a trainer can introduce distance control. This means a handler can get a dog to carry out tasks at a distance and still respond o commands at a distance. What a trainer will do is put the dog on a longer and longer lead, which gives the dog a feeling of distance but still remains attached to the trainer. The trainer can also move whilst giving the dog commands at a distance. Once mastered on a long lead the dog can then be let off the lead completely.

Leaving the Dog

This command means the dog will sit down whilst the trainer is not present. The 'down'command needs to be fully understood before the trainer can leave the dog. It needs to be introduced lowly initially at short distances and slowly he distance is increased until the trainer is out of sight from the dog, knowing the dog will remain in position.

Recall (or Come)

This command is used to bring the dog back to the trainer without any fuss. Initially, it is trained on the lead with the trainer walking in one direction and then telling the dog to come back to them. At first the lead is pulled along with the command and then over time the distance is increased before finally not using lead and the dog being called with the trainer out of sight. Each time the dog comes to the trainer it should be heavily praised.

Retrieve

This command is an important command and there are three stages to retrieval training.

Stage 1 – Hold

Initially the trainer begins by encouraging the dog the dog to take hold of a wooden dumbbell with its mouth. If the dog is reluctant to take hold, then the trainer should apply pressure to the left side of the dog's jaw. When the dog accepts the trainer pushes lightly on the dogs underjaw to reinforce the holding action. The command fetch should be linked with the dog keeping hold of the dumbbell. On each occasion the dog should be praised.

Stage 2 – Carry

When the dog can hold and leave the dumbbell, the dog needs to learn how to carry the dumbbell over a distance. Initially, this is done using the lead to apply gentle pressure, so the dog will carry the dumbbell. If the dog drops the dumbbell, the trainer should place the dumbbell back in the dog's mouth. Coupled with showing displeasure in the trainer's voice. Over time the lead can become longer and longer until the lead can be discarded and the dog will carry over a longer distance.

Stage 3 – Delivery

Once a dog understands 'carry' the final element is to learn to bring the dumbbell to the trainer. The trainer uses the command 'leave' to drop the dumbbell at the trainers feet, again this can initially be done over a short distance building it up to a much longer distance. This should include the complete hold, carry and delivery cycle.

Printed in Great Britain
by Amazon